THE HEALING TOUCH

Australian doctor Caroline Carter journeys to Southern Africa to make peace with her dying father, but arrives too late. She discovers she has inherited a cattle farm along with its manager, the mysterious Reiner Schmidt. Although determined to return to normal life in Melbourne, Caroline finds herself being won over by the farm's African employees and plagued by questions. Does she have the courage to sell her inheritance, and just what did her father intend by leaving the farm to her?

Books by Kathy George
in the Linford Romance Library:

THE HEART GOES ON
THE OTHER MAN

KATHY GEORGE

THE HEALING TOUCH

Complete and Unabridged

LINFORD
Leicester

First published in Great Britain in 2004

First Linford Edition
published 2005

British Library CIP Data

George, Kathy
  The healing touch.—Large print ed.—
Linford romance library
  1. Ranching—South Africa—Fiction
  2. Inheritance and succession—Fiction
  3. South Africa—Fiction
  4. Love stories 5. Large type books
  I. Title
  823.9′2 [F]

  ISBN 1–84395–703–5

Published by
F. A. Thorpe (Publishing)
Anstey, Leicestershire

Set by Words & Graphics Ltd.
Anstey, Leicestershire
Printed and bound in Great Britain by
T. J. International Ltd., Padstow, Cornwall

This book is printed on acid-free paper

1

Your father is dying. You must come. Reiner Schmidt — Caroline Carter stood alongside the open door of the car, her eyes skimming yet again over the words on the shiny fax paper. She flipped the page as there was another page stapled to it.

Under the letterhead of Lorentz & Kane, Attorneys at Law, she read, *Dear Miss Carter, we regret to inform you of your father's passing.*

The letter continued but she skipped the boring bits she knew by heart and went on.

In terms of the deceased's will and concerning a bequest, we would be pleased to meet with you at your earliest convenience. And there, apart from *Yours sincerely* and an illegible scrawl, the letter ended.

Caroline shifted her feet uncomfortably, the heat from the scorching ground penetrating the soles of her leather boots. Blinking away sudden tears, she scrunched the paper up into a tight ball and tossed it into the car.

After sixteen years and not a word, her father had died before she reached his side. It wasn't her fault, so why did she feel so guilty? What had he ever done for her, abandoning her when she was fourteen, leaving her to cope with an alcoholic mother and brother who would later turn to drugs?

She clenched her jaw in frustration. Why, then, she asked herself, was she in this deserted region of Africa after all this time, trying to track down her father's farm? She wanted to please him, that's why. She was still acting like a child.

Caroline lowered her head into the heated interior of the car. T-shirts and shorts littered the back seat. How had she got it into such a pickle? What had she been looking for so frantically before she came across the faxes?

Ah, Yes! Lollies.

She straightened up and glanced back down the endless dirt road, hardly distinguishable from the surrounding land with its isolated trees and sandy soil. Cutting the landscape clean across the middle was a shimmering, dancing ribbon of heat, and in the flickering heat band were two diminutive, blurry figures, two figures, she reminded herself, however small, she was counting on to rescue her.

With one leg of her sunglasses dangling from her mouth, she scrabbled again in her hot dusty luggage. Where was that bag of sweets? Were they in the holdall or the suitcase? Her hand on a warm, leather case, she hesitated as a trickle of perspiration made its way down one side of her face. Would these people take a month of Sundays to reach her?

It took another minute to locate the sweets. As luck would have it, they were at the very bottom of the case, sticky and squashed, but they would have to do. She withdrew from the car and drummed her fingers on its hot roof, gazing despairingly at the shredded tyre of the little red Volkswagen. Everything was conspiring against her.

It had been three weeks since she'd received the first fax, and it was one week before the shock had faded and she'd decided to do something about it. Another week slipped by while she arranged some leave from work and justified her decision to attend a conveniently-timed medical conference in South Africa. Then five days had elapsed before she could extricate herself politely from the conference.

While packing in her hotel room for the trip to neighbouring Namibia, she'd been given the second fax, notifying her of her father's death. She'd almost backed out then, but in the midst of her anger, she'd latched on to the one word that gave her hope — bequest.

Finally, at last, she was going to find out why her father had left them, where he had been all these years. What he had left her would be of no consequence. It would no doubt be some small memento, his watch perhaps, since it was hardly likely that he had amassed a fortune in sixteen years. But there would be a letter explaining everything, and such a letter was all she was interested in. Arriving in Namibia, she'd been prevented from seeing the solicitors, who had closed their office for lunch, and it was all the time she had to spare! It left her with no option but to travel on to the farm. Sitting around waiting was not her style.

Squinting now in the fierce sunlight, she eyed the approaching figures again. She hoped their presence meant civilisation wasn't too far away but the distances she had seen Africans walk amazed her. She shut the door and paced around the car, her mind returning to the fax.

Reiner Schmidt, the writer of the sparsely-worded fax, who was he? German, obviously, with a name like that. A neighbour, perhaps? Definitely a man of few words, accustomed to being obeyed. Elderly? No doubt.

Sweat crawled down her back. Irritably she brushed a fly away from her face and leaned in through the car window, withdrawing the keys. She could contain her impatience no longer. Besides, activity would occupy her mind.

The figures came running inquisitively when she was still some distance away, raising their hands and calling out, flashing brilliant white teeth. Two boys, they were barefoot and dressed in ragged shorts. The smaller one wore a blue T-shirt with faded wording.

Smiling, Caroline returned their greeting and offered the sweets. Chewing them noisily, they fell into step beside her, as if they'd known her all their lives. Their friendliness was infectious but the language they spoke was totally incomprehensible. At her vehicle, she pointed out the shredded front tyre and the problem of the flat spare, but they shook their heads and after a jabbered conference indicated she should accompany them.

She raised her shoulders helplessly. It would be against her judgement. In Australia, if you broke down in the outback, you stayed by your car until found. It was the accepted wisdom.

The boys began to walk away. Hastily, she slammed the boot, grabbed her leather satchel and camera from the front seat, locked up and followed.

★ ★ ★

The farm dogs loped down the driveway of the farmhouse to welcome her. They came quietly. Evidently, they knew her two companions and, apart from sniffing at the hems of her shorts, posed no threat. From the sagging, wooden garden gate, Caroline could see the farmer slouched in a wicker chair on the veranda of the sprawling homestead.

His head was tipped back, his face

covered by a khaki felt hat, his long, tanned legs ending in heavy boots, draped carelessly over the furniture. She wondered how it was that a farmer could nap in the middle of the morning. Admittedly it was hot, but not that hot as to need sleep, more the kind of heat that made you long for a cool, splashy dive into water. But this farmer chose to sleep. Somehow, it wasn't how she'd imagined farmers.

Waving away another fly, she trudged along the driveway, aware of her tired legs as she and her rescuers crossed the solitary patch of grass fronting the homestead. They halted at the steps leading up to the veranda, but the dogs went on ahead and flopped at the feet of the sleeping man.

Caroline could see into the wide, open passage of the house, but it was very quiet. Perhaps everyone else had gone to the city. Unlikely, though, as it was over one hundred kilometres away. The man lived alone then? It was possible, though she could tell from the skin of the hand that hung loosely over the armrest he wasn't old.

She cleared her throat to speak when her new friends broke into yet another string of jabber and gave her a persuasive push forward. The sudden commotion caused the farmer to jerk himself upright, his hat falling from his face as he came to his feet. His expression was one of consternation, rapidly followed by amazement. He had thick dark hair, some of the tips bleached by the sun. His face was tanned, like his legs. She couldn't see his eyes because his head was tipping back, his body swaying, his knees buckling. He was falling backwards, fainting!

He fell straight into the chair he'd been asleep in, his head jerking back, cracking against the wickerwork. Caroline cleared the polished steps two at a time, her fingers on the pulse in his neck before she thought of what she was doing. His skin was cool to the touch, but not clammy, his pulse steady but faint. She looked around, taking stock.

The veranda was clean and simply furnished with brightly-cushioned wicker chairs and a low, wooden coffee table. A collection of ragged ferns and moth-eaten pot plants in one corner attempted to give the impression of greenery. But there was nowhere to lay him out flat, and he would be awkward and heavy to move.

Without further thought, she manoeuvred his head down between his knees. Crouched beside him, she turned to the boys who crowded curiously on the steps, gaping shamelessly.

'Go, get me a blanket,' she instructed, and drew her arms around herself, shivering in an attempt to explain, feeling ridiculous.

The littler boy took off, but not into the house. Down the steps he went. Had he misunderstood her, or had she frightened him away with her shivering antics? She had never been much good at acting. She closed her eyes in annoyance as he disappeared around the back. What did it matter? She would manage.

Less than five seconds later, there was talking within the house and footsteps advancing down the passage. An African woman appeared in the doorway, clutching a dripping tea towel. She wore an ankle-length dress of bright blue and a piece of matching material contorted into something a bishop might wear was on her head.

Smiling feebly, Caroline took the proffered towel, instinctively wiping a grimy hand on it. The woman let out a string of angry words in a scolding tone but it wasn't directed at her. She spoke to the unconscious man.

Caroline was about to explain again about the blanket when the man's head moved under her touch. He was coming to. She righted his upper body slowly and looked into his eyes. They were a startling blue, pale blue embedded with flecks of a darker hue. He moved his jaw under her fingers and small, sharp pinpricks bristled against her skin. Then he said something, a few short words, totally unintelligible. She furrowed her forehead in a frown.

'Have I died?' he asked in English.

He had a deep voice with coarse, clipped consonants. In the short time she'd been in Southern Africa, Caroline's ears had become attuned to the different accents she'd encountered. He was either Afrikaans or he was German.

'No, you've just fainted.'

'I thought you were an angel.'

She'd been called lots of things in her life, often uncomplimentary, but never an angel! She smothered a smile, watching the steady rise and fall of his chest under his loose shirt. Gradually, she became aware of the assessing blue eyes which hadn't left her face. Proximity to a patient was something she wouldn't normally think twice about, but this man was not her patient, he was a stranger, a man she knew nothing about, a man who, for whatever reason, had imagined he was dead.

12

He was going to be fine, she realised. There was no earthly reason for her to be draped over his body, monitoring his heart beat! She backtracked hurriedly down the steps, stopping at the bottom, unsure of what to do next.

'Why did you do that?' he asked.

He had risen and stood at the top of the steps, taller than she had estimated, well over six feet, but on the lean side, as if he hadn't been eating properly.

'I'm a doctor. I was just trying to help.'

'That is not what I meant.'

She knew what he meant, knew intuitively he was asking her why she'd put distance between them. Why had she? What was it about him that had frightened her away? She didn't know the answer. She took a deep breath.

'Look, I'm sorry to bother you. My car . . . I had a blow-out.'

'A blow-out? Are you OK?'

He descended the stairs, concern in his voice and eyes.

'I'm fine. We walked, those boys and

I, from somewhere.'

She moved her hand vaguely in the direction of the endless dirt road.

'They rescued me, although I didn't want to leave the car. It's not something I would do back home.'

She stopped. She never gabbled, but she was gabbling now.

'Where is your car?' he asked and she raised her shoulders.

'Somewhere, that way.'

He narrowed his blue eyes as if she had a nerve interrupting his mid-morning nap. From the tiny patch of grass he called something unintelligible towards a huge, gnarled tree with white thorns as big as needles, and the little boy she had already met stepped shyly from behind it. The air escaped from Caroline's lungs. She'd been holding her breath. What was the matter with her? She was behaving like a trainee nurse on her first ward round.

The boy scampered around the corner of the house again. Why didn't they use the front door in Africa? Was it some tradition she was unaware of?

'You must be thirsty.'

She acknowledged this statement with a nod.

'Come. Sit down,' he called disappearing up the stairs and into the house. 'I'll get you a drink. Do you like lime juice?'

Caroline nodded again. Her throat was sticky from the sweets and dry, as if she was nervous. What could she possibly have to be nervous about? On the veranda, she sank down into a wicker chair, took off the camera slung around her shoulder and the small leather satchel containing her travel documents.

She could hear the muffled voices of the farmer conversing with the woman in the kitchen. She wondered if there was something wrong with him. What had caused him to faint like that? He seemed fine now. In truth, she didn't really want to know, didn't want to become involved in someone else's pain, not again. She'd been through more pain than most people. She just wanted her tyre fixed and to get on her way.

Yet there was something about this man, as if he knew everything about her, had been expecting her, but remained a mystery himself. Impatiently, she pushed some dark curls back from the damp edges of her face. She was entertaining crazy thoughts! She'd been out in the sun too long without any shade. Where was her hat anyway? The chances were she'd left it on the plane.

The drinks tinkled with ice as the man returned. Suddenly self-conscious, she picked up her camera and fiddled with it as he put down a tray with two glasses.

'Good camera,' he remarked, settling himself in a chair. 'I have one the same make, but mine is older, but it takes wonderful pictures.'

He reached over and took the camera out of her hands. His fingers were long and tanned and lacerated with thin red cuts. How had he got them into that mess? She watched him undo the case, angle the lens playfully at her and focus. She smiled from sheer habit, her eyes widening with surprise. Before she knew it, he had taken her picture, all within seconds.

'Very nice,' he murmured. 'You did not mind, did you?'

He lowered his head but there was no hiding his amusement.

'Of course, I didn't,' she murmured.

She did, but this was no time to be churlish. The heat of the little white lie crept into her face.

'You smiled as if you knew what I was doing, but your eyes, they . . . '

He shrugged as if he could not explain what it was about her eyes.

'I always smile for the camera. It's a habit.'

'A habit?'

'I have to smile a lot in my job, and sometimes I forget I don't have to smile all the time, that sometimes I can be myself.'

'What do you do that needs all this smiling?'

'I'm a doctor, but I told you that already.'

So, he didn't remember her saying that. Was he forgetful, or flustered, too, like she was?

'Ah, yes, you said so. So you have . . . ah . . . what do you call it? A good bed manner?'

The heat in her face grew. She picked up her drink, and the ice clinked against the glass.

'Bedside, I think you mean. I try to make very sick children happy,' she went on quickly, smoothing over his suggestive word.

It was an easy mistake for him to make, Caroline reasoned, just his fractured English. But why was there a glint in his eyes, as if he knew he had been provocative?

'There is something wrong with your car?' he continued as if nothing untoward had been said.

The tyre, of course! Why had she

been wasting valuable time? It was his time, too, this farmer who slept mid-morning, whose clothes hung loose on him, whose eyes were mesmerising.

'I told you I had a blow-out and the spare is flat. It's a hire car.'

She mentioned the name of the company.

'Not very professional of them. I was wondering . . . '

How did she ask? The nearest garage would be quite some distance and she was expecting him to put himself out for her. He waited for her to continue.

'I was wondering if you could help me fix it.'

'Where are you going?'

'I'm on my way to a cattle farm. It's two hundred and fifty kilometres east of Windhoek.'

'Two hundred and fifty?' he interrupted. 'What is it called?'

She ferreted in her pocket for the directions she'd received and pulled them out, spelling the farm's name out to him. He nodded and immediately pronounced the name she'd had so much trouble getting her mouth around.

'You know the farm? You knew my father, Josh Carter?'

He moved his hands roughly over the chair arms, taking his time to answer. Eventually, he said, 'I knew your father.'

She frowned. Something was bothering him. Could it be something she had said?

'Do you know a man called Reiner Schmidt?'

She pronounced the name carefully, unsure of her German.

'He faxed me in Australia, about my father.'

'I know Reiner.'

He smiled at her as if he had said something amusing.

'But not very well. Nobody knows him very well,' he admitted.

Sighing inwardly, Caroline dragged her eyes away from his smile. Oh, great! Not only was Reiner Schmidt formidable, elderly and German, but a recluse as well.

'Is the farm much farther?'

He considered the question.

'No, and it is not two hundred and fifty kilometres from Windhoek. You had better phone him and tell him you will be late.'

'I don't have a phone number for him,' she told him curtly, pushing away her drink in irritation.

She couldn't be late. She didn't have the time to be late! She got to her feet, anxious to be on her way. She wasn't prepared to wait any longer for answers to her questions.

'Haven't you got a spare tyre I could borrow or buy off you, if necessary?'

He was smiling again.

'What,' she said impatiently, 'is so funny?'

'On your nose,' he murmured. 'You have grease on your nose.'

'I have? Blast.'

She glanced down hopelessly at her dirty white shirt, creased shorts and dusty boots. This wasn't how doctors were supposed to look. Doctors were

21

supposed to be the epitome of cleanliness.

'Hold still.'

She found his hand in front of her face, and drew breath, closing her eyes as his finger rubbed at the bridge of her nose.

'It will not come off,' he admitted. 'You have blood on your lip, too.'

Casually, he picked up his hat and put it on his head.

'You must have banged your mouth on the steering-wheel.'

She stared at him, trying to make her mouth work.

'I didn't bang my face. I would remember doing something like that.'

He shrugged as he pushed back his chair.

'Let's go look at your car.'

She watched him descend the steps as she wiped her mouth with the back of her hand. Flecks of dried blood appeared on her skin. He was right, her mouth had been bleeding.

'Are you well enough to drive?' she asked.

'I am not sick,' he said over his shoulder.

'But . . . '

She searched for words to stall him. What if he fainted again? Or was the thought of being cooped up with him in a confined space holding her back?

'Don't you have to lock up?'

'Lock up?' he repeated incredulously and turned and grinned.

He had a tiny gap between his top front teeth. On someone else it might have looked unsightly, but on him it was somehow attractive.

'I mean, well, tell someone where you're going. Your wife?'

'There is no wife. There is Francina in the kitchen, my mother, overseas, and myself. And now you are here.'

She propelled her tired feet down the steps, one after the other, not looking at him, but she knew he was studying her and her grubby shirt and long brown legs. She lifted her head to say something assertive in her authoritative Dr Carter voice and met his eyes.

Curious, compelling and blue, they returned her gaze.

There were no words to say. Suddenly she realised she hadn't introduced herself, and he neither. How could they both have overlooked the niceties of manners?

'And who are you?' she asked faintly.

'Reiner Schmidt,' he said. 'What took you so long to get here?'

2

You're Reiner Schmidt?' she exclaimed as she eyed him, dismissing elderly and formidable from her mental list of Reiner Schmidt's qualities, although she wondered about reclusive.

'Why did you pretend to be someone else?'

He shoved his hands into his back pockets and rocked on the heels of his boots, observing her as if she was some dangerous species he had held captive and now freed, and was intrigued by the consequences.

'I asked you if you knew this man called Reiner Schmidt,' she persisted.

'And I said I did.'

'You said you didn't know him very well. What did you mean by that?'

No comment. She averted her head, her frustration growing by the second. What had she landed up in?

'Did you or did you not send me a fax?'

He nodded, with a firmly-closed mouth.

'And this is your farm?' she inquired.

'This is your father's farm, or was your father's farm.'

'My father's farm?'

She twisted her head, her eyes skimming over the sprawling brick farmhouse and the half-dozen cattle resting under the shade of a thorn tree.

'I told you there was a mistake with the distance.'

'If this is — was — my father's farm, what are you doing here?'

'I manage the farm, my mother and I.'

'Your mother?'

'My mother and Josh were friends.'

His mother and her father! There had been a significant pause before he said the word, friends, and his eyes looked everywhere but at her. He was telling her something, something she wasn't sure she wanted to know.

'You didn't see old man Kirkpatrick before you came out here?'

'I didn't see anyone. Who is Kirkpatrick?'

'He was your father's attorney.'

Ah, the solicitor she had failed to locate, the man who closed his city office for lunch, made himself unavailable.

'I see, and what would he have told me?'

Reiner whistled softly and ran a hand over the back of his neck.

'Many things.'

'Like?'

He shook his head and turned away.

'Let's go get your car,' he suggested.

She shot out a hand to stall him and came into contact with the warm, bare skin of his arm.

'Wait, you can't just walk off! What is it about the farm I should know?'

He murmured a reply, his eyes focused on some place in the middle distance. She tilted her head to catch the movement of his lips but for some reason he wouldn't look at her.

'Excuse me?'

'It is your farm. He left it to you.'

She opened her mouth but no words would come. Her farm? There must be some mistake.

'He couldn't have left it to me. I haven't seen him for sixteen years.'

'Well, he did. I saw the will. It is your farm.'

She blinked. It was all taking a while to sink in.

'How do I know this is true?'

'Wait here. I will get you a copy.'

He took only a minute, during which she could think no further than that there had been some ghastly mistake.

The paper the will was written on was unusually long and cumbersome, but the words were succinct and straightforward. The legal jargon stated that she, Caroline Leigh Carter, was the sole inheritor of the farm, the only stipulation being that she was to continue to employ one Reiner Anton Schmidt as farm manager until such time as the farm was disposed of, or until the said Reiner's demise, whichever came earlier. The will was dated some two months earlier, and there was no other reference to Reiner, or his mother for that matter.

She lowered the crisp parchment thoughtfully. What would she, an Australian, do with a cattle farm in Southern Africa? She almost laughed. She didn't even like meat! She pushed the damp curls back from her forehead again and caught Reiner staring at her. What would she do with this man, this man with an odd sense of humour, this man her father had employed?

'Why didn't you tell me up front who you were? Why did you pretend . . . '

She trailed off. His behaviour had been puzzling to say the least.

He shrugged, and she received a fleeting impression of big, bony shoulders under the cotton shirt.

'I was having a little fun,' he said gently.

'Fun?' Caroline's voice rose.

'It's been a while since — '

She cut him off, folding up the will with stiff fingers.

'How could you think about fun at a time like this?'

His eyes narrowed and took on a steely glint.

'Look, lady, I have been angry, too, angry when you did not turn up, when your father died without seeing you. He did not deserve that.'

He clenched his jaw and a nerve jerked along its edge.

'What is your excuse for being so late?'

'I don't need to justify things to you,' she began.

'Where is your hat?'

He stopped her continuing, obviously not interested in her excuses. Caroline shook her head, her mind in turmoil. Who could think about a hat at a time like this?

'You will need one if we are to spend any longer out here.'

'Never mind a hat,' she said. 'Where's your car?'

'Truck, and it's over there.'

She followed his rapid stride to a four-wheel drive parked in the shade of a dilapidated, corrugated-iron shed. He jerked open the passenger door and looked pointedly at her. She got in, the will still clenched in her hand.

She placed it on the space of seating between them, and struggled with the stiff and dusty seat-belt. He climbed up alongside her and watched her click her seat-belt into place as if he had never seen anyone use it before. His hung slack against the doorframe, dusty and unused. She knew there were men who had no time for the restrictions of safety, men who arrived in Casualty with surprise written all over their faces. Was he one of them?

'I'm ready now. You can go.'

He moved forward and the sun angled off the bonnet. She put on her sunglasses. Under the dashboard a dozen or so oranges rolled around, together with a pair of binoculars and a couple of empty beer cans. One

31

scratched hand steadied the wheel as he pushed at the gear lever. How had he got those cuts?

'How did my father die?' she asked after a few minutes.

'He had cancer.'

'What kind?'

'Cancer of the liver with secondaries in the lymph glands.'

Caroline knew all about the disease and its pain, knew mostly it was inoperable, that men seldom attended to it in time, but she had to ask further. There were details she had to know.

'Did he have chemotherapy?'

'It was too late.'

'How long did he suffer?'

'From start to finish, about two months.'

'Is there a grave?'

'No. Ashes. My mother took care of them.'

She held her tongue and stared out the window. Conversation with this man was an exchange of gunfire, emotionless, getting them nowhere.

With her father gone, was there any point in her being here? She had come all this way to nothing — no father, no graveside, nothing but frustration.

She glanced at the man by her side, his eyes fixed on the road ahead. The only man who could tell her anything was the strong, silent type. She slumped back against her seat. Was there anything positive to be gained out of this whole futile exercise?

If only she could find some connection with her father, something that would justify his desertion all those years ago, something to hold on to, something other than this farm. It told her nothing about her father.

Perhaps there was a letter apart from the will, a letter that would explain everything. Surely this man at her side would know.

'My father didn't leave me a letter, did he? A letter explaining all this.'

She raised an index finger and poked at the document as if it was contaminated.

'Your father? A letter?'

She nodded, but he shook his head as if the idea of her father writing anything was ludicrous. He was right. Why would her father have written to her now? He'd had years in which to get in touch with his family, and hadn't.

She sighed. She should never have come. When she got hold of the solicitor she would sign whatever papers were necessary to sell the farm and fly home, soon, tomorrow maybe. She wondered what sort of price a farm like this would fetch. It would be a tidy sum, enough to wipe out Paul's debts and at least start him on a rehabilitation programme.

They bounced along the dry, rutted roadway, dust and heat blowing in through the open window as they gathered speed. She sneezed suddenly, and sneezed again. Finding a tissue, she dabbed at her nose, and out of the corner of her eye saw Reiner's mouth lift in wry amusement. He found her sniffles amusing, did he!

The vehicle slowed as they passed

several small, compact buildings set back from the side of the road. Their occupants rested in the doorways and the meagre shade provided by a row of trees. The vehicle stopped, the engine idling, and children appeared from nowhere, crowding the window, smiling infectiously at Caroline. Grinning, she put out her hand and felt the warmth and sincerity of their welcome under her fingers.

Reiner's shirt brushed against her chest as he reached across her for the oranges. She drew back stiffly, he was so close. The blue eyes locked on hers and flickered disconcertingly for a moment, then he turned away and tossed the fruit out to the children. It seemed that everybody smiled or laughed. The African spirit was truly a wonderful thing.

'How long have you been my father's farm manager?' she asked conversationally when they set off once again.

'For as long as I've known your father.'

That was informative, Caroline thought but said nothing.

Neither of them spoke as they continued to jolt along. Caroline kept herself occupied by observing the terrain, the yellow and orange hues of the land, the blue of the sky. Long silences didn't scare her. The only thing that scared her was her patients dying on her — and snakes! But her irritation began to well up. She had a time limit and a million things about her father to learn. If this man didn't want to talk, she would have to make him!

'Are you always this chatty?' she said eventually.

'No. This is unusual for me. Are you always this inquisitive?'

'Yes, it's in my nature.'

He slowed as they reached a deserted intersection, changed gear and swung the vehicle out into the road. There must be something he could talk about, something they could discuss without charging the air with tension.

'Tell me about the farm,' she encouraged.

'It's eleven thousand hectares with just over one thousand head of cattle.'

Caroline frowned. How much was a hectare? And what would it help if she knew? She was not a farmer. The statistics meant nothing to her. Silence settled in again, so she tried a different tack.

'You said something about your mother being away. Where is she?'

'Overseas, in Germany. She'll be away for at least two months.'

He shifted in the seat as if talk of his mother made him uncomfortable.

'She went so soon after my father's death?'

'I made her go. She needed a break. There was nothing more for her to do and she needed distracting.'

In spite of her frustration, Caroline felt the first faint stirrings of sympathy for the man. He'd sent his mother away when he probably needed the extra pair of hands, not to mention the company. In her experience, not many men were capable of such unselfishness.

'She didn't want to meet me?' she ventured.

'Well, she didn't know you were coming.'

'You didn't think I would come?'

'No.'

This was not the time to tell him how close to the truth he was.

'Is this better?' he shot at her.

'Excuse me?' she replied, puzzled.

'The conversation, the chatty thing.'

'Oh, we're getting there. You must understand there are a million things I should know and only a couple of days to find them out.'

'A couple of days? You've come all this way for a couple of days?'

'I have to be back at work tomorrow week. I've already been gone two weeks including a conference I attended. I just don't have any more time.'

'So, you are not going to farm?'

'Do I look like a farmer?'

His mouth twitched and he raised an eyebrow in an expressive gesture that conveyed a thousand words, though, on reflection, she mused, a thousand words was probably a few hundred too many for him.

They crested a hill, and her little car glittered through the heat haze. Drawing up behind it, he got out and nodded his head.

'Did you lock it?'

'Of course I locked it! It has all my worldly possessions in it.'

She hurried out, sifting through her keys. Maybe he didn't lock his house when he went out, but she not only locked her house but her car as well.

'Calm down, you did the right thing.'

'I did?'

Crouched on his haunches, he was examining the shredded tyre. He squinted up at her.

'You drove with the car like this and did not roll over?'

'It's a blow-out. Nothing too serious, nothing I couldn't handle.'

He was staring at her. He appeared to have underestimated her.

'Where did you learn to drive on dirt?'

'My father taught me. He taught me to drive when I was very young, and he taught me everything there is to know about cars.'

'You were interested in cars?'

He frowned at her as he paced the perimeter of the car, checking out the remaining tyres, giving one a gentle kick.

'Uh-huh.'

'Unusual for a girl, isn't it?'

'I was an unusual child,' she said simply. 'My father treated me like a boy. He . . . '

Her voice became a whisper. Her father was dead. Somehow she had always thought he was alive somewhere in the world. It would take time to grow accustomed to the reality.

'Your father was a good man,' Reiner murmured. 'Keys? I will get the spare.'

A father who had deserted his family could never be called a good man, but she kept that comment to herself.

'I can manage,' she told him, slotting the key into the boot, aware of his eyes on her back.

Her shirt was filthy. How anyone stayed clean in this hot, dusty place was beyond her, but he seemed to manage. His blue cotton shirt was freshly laundered, his shorts recently pressed.

'Is that how you get so dirty?' he said.

'Excuse me?'

'By always insisting on doing everything yourself.'

'I know then the job gets done properly.'

'You mean you trust no-one else.'

An acute observation, certainly and one for which she had no reply without going into her family history, her alcoholic mother, her drug-addicted brother.

He worked quickly, picking up the spanner and tackling the obstinate nuts she'd had no success with. Watching him, her eyes were drawn to the cuts on his fingers.

'How did you hurt your hands like that?'

'I had a fight with a wildcat.'

'Sure you did.'

He stopped what he was doing and levelled his eyes at her. She had been glared at plenty of times before by some intimidating men with a trail of letters behind their names, but Reiner's hard look of antagonism surpassed all of theirs put together. Formidable — the word flashed through her mind again.

'OK, OK,' she back-pedalled, trying to settle her pulse rate, 'so you did have a fight with a — a — '

'Wildcat. This is a farm,' he reminded her impatiently, as he heaved the spare tyre out of the boot. 'You get wild things on farms.'

'Like yourself,' Caroline muttered.

He balanced the tyre against the bumper and banged the boot shut, but she knew he had heard her. What a big mouth she had! She waited, taut with tension, wondering what biting remark he was going to shoot at her next. Instead, he gave her a broad grin, and she felt the anxiety ease from her body.

He had a very attractive smile. It showed the slight gap in his front teeth, reminding her of its sensuality.

'So, the lady does have a sense of humour. I was beginning to think you were not the daughter of your father.'

Heat fanned into Caroline's cheeks. She lowered her gaze and scuffed at the sand with her boot. How did the man succeed in embarrassing her?

Settling the tyre into the back of the truck, he said conversationally, 'Have you still got your camera, or have you mislaid it again?'

'I've still got it. Why?'

Caroline turned and followed his line of sight. At the fence, observing them quietly while it chewed on a mouthful of grass, stood a huge antelope. Grabbing her camera off the front seat, she picked her way excitedly across the sand. The animal, his stunning, symmetrical black and white coat like something out of mediaeval times, backed away as she approached. Then he stopped and snorted, as if to say, this

43

far and no farther. She paused, fiddled with buttons and dials and focused.

'Wait.'

A grease-stained hand settled on top of the camera and pushed it down gently.

'You do not want all that fencing in the picture, do you?'

'Of course I don't, but if I go any closer, I'll scare him off.'

At close quarters, she glanced up at Reiner, seeing for the first time the lines on his suntanned face. She had put him at roughly her age, early thirties. Perhaps he was older than she thought.

'If you are quiet, he will be fine,' he muttered, propelling her forward.

She balanced the camera on the fence wires, steadying her hand. Why had he pushed her away like that? She focused as the animal pawed the ground, dust clouding his hooves as the shutter clicked. It was the perfect shot. If nothing else came of this trip, at least she would have a fantastic picture.

In under five minutes her luggage

was loaded up in the back of his truck and they were returning to the farm. Caroline sat quietly. If she said nothing, perhaps the man would talk of his own accord.

'Why did you take so long to get here?' he said eventually.

'I was in South Africa, attending a medical conference.'

'It is not the normal place for Australians, is it?'

'No,' she said and drew out the word, wondering how much to tell him. 'I am interested in helping countries where they don't have the facilities, or the financial back-up.'

'Do you go to conferences often?'

'Two or three times a year.'

'And you do not get sick of them?'

'No. I like to help where I can, especially in countries where they don't have the know-how or the finances.'

'You like to help?' He frowned. 'You were in South Africa not to learn anything new, but to teach them something?'

'In a nutshell, yes. I have to be prepared to give of my time and knowledge if I want promotion.'

'You want a promotion?'

'I didn't say that.'

'It is what you did not say that tells me what you mean.'

She sighed.

'Well, yes, I do want a promotion.'

If she didn't get the promotion and the raise in salary that went with it, she would have trouble finding the money to help Paul.

'Where is your brother?'

The question coincided neatly with her thoughts, but she had difficulty with it. How much did she tell Reiner about Paul? How much did he already know?

'He's in Melbourne. He's not too good at travelling long distances.'

She gazed out the window at the desolate landscape, alarmed to find her eyes filling with tears. What was the matter with her? She couldn't possibly be grieving for her father, could she? Not after all this time.

3

Reiner stumbled, his desert boots clattering, his legs feeling leaden, as he crossed the brass plating at the front doorway of the farmhouse. It was happening again.

He peeled off his shirt, halfway to his bedroom, and threw it, damp with perspiration, into the laundry basket. Collapsing on his bed, he flung his arms above his head. What did these sudden sweats and lethargy mean, and when would they pass? What kind of sickness did he have?

Dr Carter would know, but he was damned if he would ask her. His sickness wasn't a priority. There were other things he needed to know which were far more important, and there were only so many questions he could ask. For instance, what was she going to do with his farm? His farm? He had to get that thought clear out of his head. It might have been going to be his farm once, but it belonged to her now.

For the umpteenth time since Josh's death, he wondered what in the world had possessed the man to bequeath the farm to her. Blood was thicker than water, but it puzzled him why the son never came into it. Why would a man leave a farm to a daughter when he had a son?

She said she wasn't going to farm; it would be over his dead body. He smiled faintly. The way he felt right now, it was a possibility he hadn't counted on. He screwed up his eyes. As if he had a choice in the matter, but how was he going to get around to telling her the farm was actually his? If his bad-tempered brute of a father hadn't gambled it away, he would have inherited it as a matter of course, and Josh would never have come into the picture. Yet without Josh, who knew where he and his mother would be today? He had a lot to be thankful for.

Lying on his bed usually relieved the headaches he had been suffering from, but today, his thoughts circled painfully around an image of Caroline's face, as if everything he ever did from now on would revolve around her.

At the edge of the chaos, there was a sound like a scream. He raised himself on one elbow, the effort making his head throb. Had he actually heard someone call his name? There was only one person who would yell out for him — the new owner of his farm.

He heaved his weary body upright and swung his feet off the bed slowly, regretting his decision to house her in the guest quarters set apart from the farmhouse. Before she left, his mother had prepared the bedroom adjoining his, but one look at Josh's daughter this morning instinctively told him that bedroom would be a bad idea. Why, he still wasn't sure.

By the time he crossed the small front lawn and reached her room, his head felt close to bursting. He knocked on the door, but after a second's silence simply pushed it open. Her leather suitcase gaped open on the floor, clothes erupting haphazardly from its depths. The dirty white shirt she'd been wearing was thrown over a chair, the khaki shorts and some silky underwear abandoned on the rug where she had stepped out of them. He averted his eyes.

'Yes?' he called, one arm braced against the doorway.

He would not use her name, and become familiar with its owner. He would keep his distance from her. He stepped into the room. The overhead fan whirred, its noise increasing his pain. Painstakingly, he turned the knob, and the fan slowed. A muffled noise came from behind the closed bathroom door.

'In here,' a stage whisper came.

'What is it?'

'Just get in here.'

The words were gritty as if she spoke through clenched teeth.

Hesitating at the door to the en-suite, Reiner glanced at his bare chest. He had forgotten to put on a shirt!

'You want me to enter?' he asked tentatively.

'Yes!'

'Are you dressed?'

The terse answer was a word he expected her to know but not to use. He shoved open the door. Wide-eyed, she was backed up against the wall of the shower, her dark hair curling damply around her face, her hands clutching the towel so tightly across her chest the whites of her knuckles showed.

'What is it?'

Barely moving, as if the wall would fall down if she did, she inclined her head in the direction of the toilet behind the door.

'Over there.'

'Why are you whispering?'

He broke off as he widened the door and peered behind it. He stifled a snort of laughter which he knew she wouldn't appreciate.

'I wondered where he had got to.'

'He?' she squeaked. 'You know this . . . this . . . '

'I know this snake,' he said softly.

He crouched down and with the utmost care unwound a sleepy brown snake from around the curvature of the toilet bowl.

'He keeps away the rats and meerkats, and is very valuable. We go back a long way.'

Straightening up, he could see from her facial expression that nothing he said was getting through to her. Making a narrow platform with his left arm against his bare chest, he deposited the bulk of the snake's body on to it.

'Boof, meet Josh's daughter,' he said conversationally, taking his eyes off his charge and glancing at her.

Her eyes and shape of her nose were startlingly similar to Josh's, but that was where it ended. The rest of her was nothing like Josh, nothing like him at all. That continued to surprise him and cause him considerable consternation.

'Boof is a mole snake,' he said inanely, as if she would care.

For once, she had nothing to say, but he could see a pulse hammering in her slender neck which told him she was terrified.

'Boof is harmless.'

'I don't care whether he gets paid for sleeping on the job or whether it's just an occupational hazard, just get him out. I never want to see him again.'

She closed her eyes and her chest heaved against the fluffy towel. Reiner stroked Boof's scaly head absently, reluctant to leave, enjoying the occasion. It had been an awful long time since he had been in the company of a woman. Lorna had put paid to that.

'I said, take him away.' Her tone was icy.

He dragged his gaze back to Boof, cradled against his chest, silent, uncomplicated, not like women.

'Mr Schmidt — ' she began haughtily, using the form of address his father had always insisted upon.

'Do not call me that,' he said harshly and winced, remembering too late his thumping head.

'Are you leaving or are you going to stand there all day and stare at me?'

Taken aback, he narrowed his eyes. What a little upstart. He didn't think he'd been staring at her.

'Don't hiss,' he reprimanded. 'You will make Boof crazy.'

Open-mouthed, she eyed him through the clear glass of the shower screen. He had succeeded in silencing her a second time and controlled an urge to smirk.

'I was thinking . . . I need to see a doctor,' he said quickly.

An inquiring expression came over her face.

'What are your consulting hours?' he continued, tongue-in-cheek. 'Or do I need an appointment?'

'You'll need — '

'A referral?' he interrupted.

'You'll need to give me a urine sample,' she told him. 'First thing tomorrow morning, although, of course, I may be gone by then.'

He blinked, then left slowly through the doorway, the snake's long body swinging at his side.

She had a busy mouth with a habit of surprising him with her words. If he wanted to manoeuvre the farm from her clutches and retain his pride, he would have to see to that mouth — and he did not have much time.

4

Caroline dressed quickly, slipping her damp feet into flat, leather sandals and pulling a brush through her wet hair. Lunch was at twelve-thirty, and it was now twelve twenty-five. She would not be late for lunch, she told herself sternly, even if it was with a man who counted snakes amongst his friends.

In the dining-room, Reiner had his back to her at a sideboard. Damp hair fringed the collar of a fresh white shirt. He had showered, too. He was an attractive man, she decided, but although the suntan gave him a healthy aura, she was sure he was ill. But with what? And, more importantly, was it infectious?

Alerted by the noise of her entrance, he glanced up into the mirror, holding her gaze for just that moment longer than necessary. There was something altogether too mesmerising about those blue eyes. He closed the cabinet door and the muted sound of music began to filter through the room. It took her aback. She couldn't remember when she'd last had lunch to the accompaniment of classical music. Mostly, she ate something wet and fibrous between slices of what the hospital canteen called bread while she read the newspaper or caught up on paperwork.

'Please, sit down. Would you like a drink?'

She took her place at the table. The shiny antique timber was laid with white plates, starched napkins and silver cutlery.

'Thank you, a drink would be nice. Something light, like the lime juice you gave me earlier.'

'You wouldn't prefer a beer?'

'A beer? I drink only occasionally, usually never. Sometimes I'll have the odd one.'

She was doing it again — gabbling! How did she stop?

'Josh taught me to enjoy a good wine.

He drank and enjoyed it.'

He filled a glass of juice and pushed it over to her, then ran his fingers slowly along the curved rim of the chair's back.

'He said your mother was an alcoholic. Is that why you don't drink?'

She brought her fidgeting hands to the edge of the table, forcing herself to still them. So he knew about her mother. What else did he know?

'I feel I'm at a disadvantage here, Reiner. You seem to know all about me, yet I know nothing about you.'

The overhead fan whirred, filling the silence.

'There must be something you can tell me,' she encouraged. 'How long have you known my father?'

He pulled out a chair opposite and slid into it, brushing his boot against her foot. Startled by the sudden contact, she withdrew her feet hastily.

'Reiner?' she prodded.

'Please, help yourself. We eat simply but there's plenty.'

There was — plates of sliced, cold meat, fresh, delicious-smelling bread, butter, conserves, at least three different cheeses and fruit. For two people, it was quite a spread. She reached for a bread roll, giving up on her quest for personal details.

Instead she inclined her head and asked, 'What is this music?'

'It is one of my favourites, a German opera, called Lohengrin. Generally I am not a lover of opera, but this one . . . ' He shrugged. 'Your father enjoyed it very much.'

'My father liked opera?'

'You do not remember?'

'I don't recall him listening to music much at all. It was a long time ago.'

'He loved opera, if you want to know.'

'There are things I want to know.'

She paused. She needed to be tactful.

'I understand from what you say that my father and your mother were . . . '

'Lovers.'

The word confirmed her suspicions.

59

Their parents had been more than friends. The revelation made the situation difficult. She had a certain responsibility towards Reiner and his mother.

'In the will you showed me this morning, there appears to be no provision made for your mother. Did my father provide adequately for her?'

He rested his fork on his plate and shook his head.

'What difference would that make to you?' he said, but she knew he thought it was none of her business.

'I am assuming my father loved your mother. That is what you have told me. If he hasn't adequately provided for her, I need to rectify the situation.'

'Do you have the funds to do that?'

She shrugged.

'I really need to meet with the lawyers, but I could split the proceeds from the sale of the farm.'

His fork clattered on the tabletop, cutting her off.

'This is not the time for such a

discussion,' he said curtly. 'Lunch is the time to appreciate food. Why are you not eating?'

His reaction and the question took her by surprise. She looked at her plate which was empty. On her side plate, a crumbled bread roll stared back at her. How had she become so distracted? She helped herself to salad and cheese and surreptitiously watched him as he picked at his food. For a big man he ate a miniscule amount. It was time to get to the bottom of whatever was ailing him.

'Have you got a sore throat?' she inquired.

'No.'

'But you have a headache. Any other symptoms?'

'How do you know I have a headache?'

'I can see pain in your eyes. I'm surmising it's a headache.'

'I don't want to talk about it, not while I am eating.'

'But you're not eating. As a doctor, I

can tell you this is a good time to talk. You're distracted by the food and will find it easier to unburden yourself.'

'Unburden myself? Do you use this fancy terminology with all your patients, or just the ones you try to impress?'

'Most of my patients are children. Of course, I don't use those words with them, they wouldn't understand.'

She frowned as she picked out a cherry tomato with her fingers and popped it into her mouth. Why did he think she needed to impress him?

'I'm not the kind of woman who tries to impress people. What you see is what you get,' she told him. 'I see no point in pussy-footing around. We're both grown-ups.'

'Pussy-footing?'

She began an explanation, but he wasn't listening. Clearly, the moving bulge of the small tomato in her cheek fascinated him. She would have to do something about it. She crunched down, and an inelegant splattering of pips flew out of her mouth, followed by a dribble of cool red juice down her chin. She closed her eyes, and muttered something unrepeatable. Chewing rapidly, gulping down the mouthful, she jerked out her napkin, dipped one end into a nearby water jug and dabbed helplessly at the spreading red stain on her cotton shirt. How many more clean shirts did she have?

'Lovely tomatoes,' she said lamely, shuffling her napkin back on her lap and feeling the warmth of her reddened cheeks.

Motionless, he stared at her, a smile playing about the corners of his lips. She tried again.

'Someone in this desert knows how to grow tomatoes.'

He straightened his back, and she caught a hint of pride in his voice as he said, 'I grow them.'

'You grow them?'

'What do you think I do with my time?'

'I wouldn't have a clue, but I would have thought you'd be fairly busy.'

'You know what they say? There is nothing much to do as long as the windmill and the bull are doing their jobs.'

Caroline's eyes widened, and the smile that had been hovering about Reiner's mouth could no longer be contained. With his shoulders shaking and his hand knocking the tabletop in helpless appreciation, he gave in to a convulsion of laughter.

She picked up the silver napkin ring she'd been given and tapped it irritably on the table. Lunch wasn't working out the way she had planned. In fact, nothing was working out the way she had planned!

'This morning, grease on your nose, and your shirt, and now, the tomato. Do you always make such a mess of yourself?'

'I'm afraid so,' she said wryly. 'Clumsiness, like curiosity, is in my nature. I should have been a boy.'

'A boy? I think not.'

His laughter died as he tilted his head

and assessed her.

She didn't know where to look. What had they been talking about? She needed to get the conversation back on level ground, but he was quicker on the uptake.

'Farming,' he reminded her gently, 'do you know anything about farming?'

'Absolutely nothing.'

'But do you want to learn? I can teach you, you know, and make a farmer out of you.'

She shook her head adamantly.

'I have a job back home in Melbourne, a very good job. I have no intention of becoming a farmer.'

'Ah, yes, the promotion.'

Uneasy, she shifted in her seat. How had the conversation reverted to her so quickly? She reached for the lime juice and refilled her glass.

'We've talked enough about me, Reiner. It's your turn. You have a bad headache. I gather you've had it for some days. What else can you tell me?'

Pushing himself away from the table,

he rose and, without a word, moved his fingers over his shirt buttons.

'What are you doing?'

'You seem determined to detect what is wrong with me, Doctor Carter. Do you want to examine me?'

Without waiting for an answer, he peeled off the shirt and slung it over a chair. He had well-developed shoulders like a swimmer and honey-coloured skin. Naked to the waist, he appeared taller, if that was possible.

'Well?'

She pushed her chair away from the table with some effort.

'Sit down,' she ordered, her voice belying the chaos she felt inside her body. 'I have to get my bag and wash my hands.'

She was glad of the chance to escape the room, calm herself and put things in perspective. She couldn't fathom the man out, he was so unpredictable.

Her doctor's bag wasn't in the guest quarters when she got there. She was perplexed. She remembered seeing

Reiner carry it in from the truck. So, where could it be?

'One of your little friends probably has it,' Reiner suggested on her return. 'You will find it back in your room in a couple of hours, as if it has never been touched.'

'I hope not,' she said, running a hand worriedly through her curls. 'It has some important gear in it.'

He reached for his shirt.

'So you won't be examining me?'

The words were casual, but his voice carried an unmistakable sound of hope. Perhaps he was as nervous of the ordeal as she was. In that case . . .

'I don't see why not,' she said flatly.

Seating him in a chair opposite hers, she got it over with. She could find nothing wrong with him. He was perhaps too thin and had a throbbing headache. He admitted to symptoms of lethargy, but without a blood test there was little to go on. She put down the teaspoon she had used to examine his throat, careful not to contaminate her fingers.

'I think you're generally exhausted and traumatised by my father's death, and you haven't been eating properly. You probably lost interest in food as a result of everything else.'

He waited, as if he expected more, and so she went on. There were some patients with whom you never held anything back.

'Then again, you might have something more serious.'

'What?'

'Glandular fever. It's usually restricted to young adults, teenagers. The symptoms are a sore throat, temperature, headaches and lethargy.'

Talking professionally calmed her · completely. It was business as usual. She was the doctor, and he was no more than a patient.

'For that, you'd need to have blood and urine samples sent off for testing, and you'll need to attend to that as soon as possible.'

'And what if I have got glandular

fever? Who will run the farm while I'm recovering?'

'I don't know. There must be someone who can help you. A neighbour, perhaps?'

She stood and pushed in her chair.

'Could I get a cup of coffee somewhere? I usually have about six a day and I'm starting to get withdrawal symptoms,' she asked.

'Coffee?'

He forced out the word, clearly annoyed by her reluctance to get involved.

'In the kitchen. Ask Francina.'

She turned to go, but he clutched at her hand unexpectedly.

'Wait! Why did you come here if you are so uninterested in the farm and everything else?'

'Because I made a promise, and I never break promises,' she said, pulling away without success.

'To whom did you make a promise?'

She didn't reply. Her promise to her mother on her deathbed wasn't the only reason she had come. There was also her curious nature. And how could she tell Reiner all she wanted to do was bawl her father out? What sort of woman would he think she was? And why did she care what he thought of her?

His fingers moved against her hand. She opened her mouth but couldn't speak, intensely aware of his warm, rough hand clasped in hers, of his gaze drifting over her mouth. He wanted to kiss her!

The idea was ludicrous, but appealing. Was she going mad?

She drew herself upright, yanked her hand out of his, and fled.

5

Francina stood at the kitchen sink, her hands submerged in soapy water. Turning, she gazed shyly at Caroline.

Caroline felt for her. All that dress, in this heat. Pushing her sweaty palms down her skirt, Caroline tucked away a wayward curl. Somehow the anger she expected refused to come. She didn't feel angry, but she did feel confused.

Coffee — that was what she needed to get her on the straight and level again. She opened her mouth to voice her request, then closed it again. Coffee was a simple drink, delicious and comforting, but now a major problem through lack of a common language. Next time she went into the city she would acquire a dictionary. But would it be German or some African language? She had no idea.

She lifted an imaginary cup to her

lips and looked hopefully at Francina. She had stunning deep-brown eyes, Caroline noted. They were large and set wide apart in her clear ebony skin.

Francina took her sudsy hands out of the sink and wiped them on the front of her apron, when it became obvious the woman was pregnant! The realisation took Caroline by surprise. She wondered how far gone she was. With all those flounces on her dress it was impossible to tell. Saying something Caroline didn't understand, Francina crossed the floor to the fridge and drew out a bottle of water.

Caroline shook her head. She glanced around the large country-style kitchen for assistance. Everything was spotless but bare, the normal kitchen paraphernalia hidden from view. There wasn't a canister or coffee mug in sight, nothing to assist her. She tried again. She poured liquid into an imaginary cup and raised it to her lips.

'Coffee?'

Francina shook her head. Smiling,

she remained silent. Caroline bent down and opened a cupboard, looking for a familiar jar, a percolator or a plunger, but the cupboard was neatly stacked with white and gold-trimmed dinner plates, side plates and dessert bowls.

She opened another cupboard, and another and another. It was only when she had all the cupboards open that she stopped. Francina leaned against the sink, shaking her head, an amused expression on her face. Caroline smiled back. Francina began to giggle, an infectious, musical giggle half-hidden behind a hand. Caroline started to laugh, too. She couldn't help herself.

'I thought you were getting a coffee?'

Reiner had appeared in the doorway.

'I'm trying to!' Caroline told him, taking a wobbly breath.

'You mean all this time you have not got as far as the coffee? What have you been doing?'

He eyed her from his position against the doorjamb.

'Getting to know the locals. Some of them are friendly,' she added pointedly. 'Please tell Francina what I need.'

He uttered a short, sharp sentence and comprehension dawned in Francina's eyes, but not without a fresh burst of giggles. Caroline tried not to look at her.

'Thank you,' she said graciously. 'When is the baby due?'

He raised his eyebrows.

'You can tell, with all that dress?'

'Of course.'

'The baby is due any day now.'

A sick man and a woman about to give birth at any time — what had she walked into? She studied Francina as she drew back a small countertop roller door, revealing a neatly-hidden kettle and coffee machine.

'It's none of my business, but she doesn't look full term. Does she carry small babies?'

'I have no idea. This is her first.'

Caroline groaned inwardly. The scenario was not improving, but there was

74

no point standing around bemoaning her fate. She might as well make herself useful. She selected a tray from a narrow slot between cupboards and brushed past Reiner on her way to collect the dirty plates from the dining-room, returning laden a moment later.

'After lunch, Francina is to rest,' she instructed over her shoulder as she piled plates into the sink of soapy water. 'In fact, both of you are to rest.'

'Yes, Doctor.'

Ignoring his sarcasm, she went down the passage a second time, hearing his footsteps behind her as he followed. She turned abruptly and raised her hand.

'Stop,' she said. 'I can do this. Until we know what's wrong with you, I don't want you doing anything you don't have to.'

But he didn't stop. He pushed against the flat of her hand until she could feel his heart beating under her palm.

'This is my home,' he said firmly. 'I will do what I want.'

On the point of reminding him that it wasn't his home any longer, Caroline dropped her hand. Her heart palpitated with a pressure she didn't think had anything to do with her anger. Tight-lipped, she stalked down the passage. She wasn't in Australia. The choice words she might have spat out to a colleague in such circumstances would never do here.

When the table was cleared, she waited at the french doors in the kitchen, enjoying the aroma of percolating coffee filling the air, and the view across the land to the low, distant hills, shimmering in the heat. After a minute, Reiner joined her. If he was going to stand there, she might as well make him talk.

'Why did you pretend your English wasn't very good this morning?'

'Ah, the bedside word,' he said. 'I cannot resist a little fun. And your face,' he went on, grinning, 'it is worth a thousand pictures.'

She frowned. How did he manage to get his English so cock-eyed that it made sense? A face worth a thousand pictures? The idea was original.

'You told me you look after very sick children. What exactly is it you do?' he went on.

'I'm a paediatric doctor, in charge of the intensive care unit. Most of the children I look after have cancer.'

'And if you get your promotion, what is it you will do then? Will you still care for your children?'

'No,' she said curtly, thinking of the administration and bureaucracy the position involved.

'What is the point of this promotion?'

She didn't answer. Money was the only point, and she couldn't admit to that. She was giving up the practical doctoring she knew and loved for money, money for Paul's rehabilitation. How could she think that money would compensate for the lack of contact with her patients? She clenched her jaw. It was no good thinking about it. It had to be done.

'Where did you learn to speak English?' she asked, diverting her thoughts.

'I learned to speak English first at school, then later at university.'

'You went to university?'

She couldn't keep the surprise out of her voice. There was no earthly reason why he shouldn't have attended, but what a thing to say! She went on, not giving him a minute to dwell on her mistake.

'Does your mother speak English, too? She must have, in order to communicate with my father. I can't imagine my father learning German.'

She was jabbering again.

'Yes, I went to university and have a degree in agriculture and economics. Imagine that! And, yes, my mother speaks English. Your father never learned German,' he told her. 'He was too . . . too . . . '

He stopped, then spoke again, his

voice a murmur.

'Lovers do not need language to communicate. You should know that. Have you never been in love?'

Her hand was shaking when she took her coffee from Francina. Avoiding Reiner's eyes, she mumbled a barely comprehensible excuse about resting herself and made a quick exit. In her room, she gulped at her coffee, burning her tongue. She had deserved that little outburst, but his words cut her to the quick.

She had been in love, and all it had taught her was that the only person she could trust was herself. Maybe she was callous and unfeeling sometimes, but she was only looking out for herself, protecting her feelings. She put down her empty cup and her gaze fastened on her doctor's bag, exactly where it should have been a half hour before. She frowned, not understanding. How could she have overlooked it? It had definitely not been there earlier.

She sat down on the edge of the bed,

tired, and hauled the bag towards her. Clicking it open, she went through its contents but there was nothing of importance missing. Listless, she lay back and stretched out on the bed. How could Reiner suggest she had never been in love? Did she really present so uncaring an exterior?

When she awoke it was after four. With no sign of Reiner, she went for a walk down the dusty driveway and back, making the acquaintance of the farm employees she had met briefly in the morning. News of her arrival had spread and everybody wanted to talk to her or clasp her hand. It was oddly touching.

By the time she returned, the sun was setting and then somebody seemed to turn out a light. Caroline had never seen darkness fall so quickly. She made her way to the house for dinner, noticing that none of the inside lights had been turned on although all the doors and windows were flung wide to let out the heat of the day.

The four-wheel drive was still parked alongside the dilapidated barn, but Reiner was not around. There was no-one in the kitchen and no evidence of any prepared meal left for her. With little to eat at breakfast or lunch, Caroline was hungry. Roaming the sprawling farmhouse, she began to worry. Perhaps his condition had worsened. Perhaps he had fainted again, and banged his head. Concerned, she ventured into rooms that she had avoided up to now.

The light in the bedroom where she found him was gloomy and growing darker by the minute, but the form on the bed was unmistakable.

'Reiner?'

Whispering, she leaned across his body and put her palm to his forehead. It was cool, but she could see he was very pale.

'How are you feeling?' she asked gently.

He opened his eyes, blinking in surprise.

'I have been better.'

She sat down slowly on the edge of his bed. Calmly, she picked up one of his hands. They were slender, long-fingered hands, but the lacerations made them rough. After a minute, she tried again.

'Have you had a tetanus shot for these scratches?'

'No.'

His attention wasn't on her. He was watching his hand in hers.

'Reiner, you're crazy! You could get — '

'I know what I could get, but what could I do? Nip off to the doctor?'

He was one of those men with no regard for his own safety.

'Tomorrow, you will get a tetanus shot if I have to drag you there, and at the same time, you can have a blood test in case you have glandular fever.'

'How did I get this, what you call it, glandular fever?'

'I don't know if it is glandular fever. Your symptoms aren't typical.'

'But how would I get it?'

She wanted to evade the question, but her brain was clogged. What was she doing in his bedroom, perched on his bed? She took a deep breath, and he watched her with shadowed eyes. She was glad of the dark for some strange reason.

'It's usually contracted by kissing.'

She stumbled over the word.

'Have you been . . . I mean, is there someone you . . . '

'No. Your diagnosis must be wrong.'

'I don't do wrong,' she told him sharply, the accusation bringing her to her senses. 'It's more likely it's slipped your mind.'

'Kissing someone is not something I would forget.'

She lowered her gaze and saw with dismay that his hand was still clasped in hers.

Her thumb slipped rhythmically across its surface caressing the soft hollow of skin between his thumb and index finger, a Dr Carter bedside habit.

She jerked her hand out of his without thinking, voicing the first thing that came into her head.

'Do you surf?'

The question obviously surprised him as much as it did her. He took his time answering.

'I used to,' he said at last, 'when I was a kid, a long time ago. What made you ask?'

Now she was in a predicament. How did she explain that she could envisage him straddling a surfboard, gazing at the incoming swell for that perfect wave, without sounding nuts?

'Intuition,' she told him.

The answer seemed to satisfy him.

'I can take you to the coast later, when I am better. The sand dunes are some of the highest in the world.'

'I'm not staying. I just don't have the time,' she said a little too fiercely.

'The time for what?' he asked, a sparkle in his eyes.

'You know what I mean.'

'Do I?'

He raised himself on an elbow, levelling his very blue eyes with hers.

'What are you so afraid of?' he asked softly.

Rising from the bed, she backed away.

'I'm not afraid of anything,' she said stoutly.

But she was. She was afraid that he would leave the bed and follow her across the room. She wanted him to, and that thought frightened her more than anything.

'Oh, yes?'

'OK! Snakes, and patients dying on me. Does that about cover it? Now for dinner,' she said, changing the subject briskly. 'I'm starving, and you must eat, too, whether you are hungry or not.'

She moved across the floorboards of the darkened room as, behind her, he switched on his bedside lamp, lighting her way. Her footsteps stopped. One wall of his simple but adequately-furnished room was filled with photographs, from the floor to virtually the ceiling.

Several of them were landscapes,

stark and bold, filled with the colours she had seen out on the land. One or two, of dying cattle, their ribs exposed to the heat of the day, were realistically brutal. One was black and white, a photograph of an older man leaning against a weathered fence post, squinting into the sun, a bemused expression on his face.

Startled, she stepped back. It was her father! Alongside him, with her head on his shoulder, was a petite, pretty blonde woman — Reiner's mother? Her eyes travelled the length of the wall and back. The display was stunning. He knew how to compose a picture, there was no doubt of that, but there were no photographs of any other people, she noted, no pictures of his own father.

Where, she wondered, was his own father. What had happened to him?

'I told Francina to go home and rest as ordered. I will get up and cook us something,' he was saying.

She turned. Immersed in the photographs, she had forgotten he was there.

'Stay where you are, I can manage. But between you and Francina, how are you going to manage?'

Immediately, she regretted the question because she had no intention of getting involved. She should have. This was now her farm, a fact she was having difficulty coming to terms with. She glanced back at the picture of her father. Before she knew it, she had lifted the frame off the wall and was cradling the image in her hands.

What was she doing? The sooner she saw her father's solicitor and sorted out this mess, the better.

'I was coming to that,' he said, swinging his legs over the edge of his bed and sitting upright.

'We have a trailer-load of cattle to get to market tomorrow.'

Tomorrow? We? Before she could voice those objections, he said, 'I will need your help.'

What about what she needed? She needed a new tyre, a solicitor and a real estate agent. Hastily, she jammed the photograph back on the hook.

'Can't you miss the market, just for once?'

'The next one is six weeks away,' he explained patiently. 'We need the money.'

Caroline opened her mouth to protest, then closed it again. They needed the money? She edged to the door. She didn't want to know why they needed the money. The less she knew, the better.

'So, we will go together, yes?'

He gazed across the room at her and his eyes filled with pain.

'Josh and I would have gone together. It will be the first time I have done the trip without him.'

In the morning, she hurried out of her room on her way to breakfast and almost fell over someone in her way, small, black and solemn-faced.

She stopped stuffing her linen shirt into the waistband of her denim skirt and glanced at the little boy.

'Hello,' she said. 'I don't think we've

been properly introduced. I'm Caroline.'

He drew his thin strips of fuzzy eyebrows together in a frown. She pointed to herself.

'Caroline.'

He got the message. He pointed to his chest and reeled off a name, not a syllable of which she understood. Carefully, she pulled at his fraying shirt where the maker's wording was coming to shreds.

'Nike,' she said, smiling.

Awkwardly, but with determination, he repeated the name.

'So far, so good,' she said under her breath. 'Now, what's the problem?'

He gave her a shy smile, showing the edges of several dazzlingly white teeth, and held out a brown-skinned arm. Her gaze fixed on the ends of two brightly-coloured band-aids she thought she recognised. She crouched down and turned over the arm. Exclaiming softly, she studied the underside.

'What have you done to yourself?'

Then, 'So that's where my bag went.'

He gave her an earful of African, but she shook her head in frustration. He stopped short. He was quick on the uptake.

She took him into the bathroom and seated him alongside the basin. Gently, she prised the ends of the band-aids from his skin and peeled them from his arm. The wound was deep and oozing blood. She could see at a glance it needed stitches, but she wasn't carrying any local anaesthetic.

Perhaps if he could keep the wound clean and himself quiet, she could obtain some materials in the city and sew it up when she returned. She filled the basin with warm water, making a mental note to pick up a suitable anaesthetic and some needles, then she stopped herself.

Just yesterday, she had declared she was leaving today. But there was no way she could leave when he needed her help. And, she reasoned, she was tied down by a flat spare tyre and a truckful of cattle, at least until tomorrow. What would one day more matter?

She cleaned and dressed the wound, binding it expertly and firmly with a bandage. The little boy uttered not a word of complaint, his large dark eyes fixed trustingly upon her. Plastering a fresh Mickey Mouse band-aid over the dressing to wear as a badge of bravery, she made the motions of sleeping so he would get the idea that he must rest.

'Tomorrow morning,' she told him, 'you must come by so I can check my handiwork.'

Although he didn't understand English, she hoped he would get the gist of what she said. En route to the door, he picked up one of her opal earrings lying on the coffee table, and turned it over in his hand, mesmerised by its ever-changing colours.

She let him study it, but after a minute, she said, 'No,' and pointed to the table. 'Put it down.'

He did, but just to make sure he understood her, she gave him a mouthful of what would happen if he touched her things again, drawing a finger across her throat to illustrate her point. He found her animations very amusing. In fact, he laughed with such hilarity she could see every one of his stunning teeth. Piqued, but smothering her own amusement behind pursed lips, she gave him a gentle shove towards the door and closed it firmly behind him.

The door didn't lock, or rather, it had a lock but no key. She looked around in exasperation. How was she going to ensure he didn't return to fiddle with her things again? In the end, she put the opals at the bottom of her suitcase and locked it. Her doctor's bag didn't have a lock, but she pushed it under the bed where she thought it was well hidden.

Then, clutching her camera and wallet of travel documents she made her way quickly to the house, following the smell of fresh coffee to the dining-room. As she helped herself to a cup, she saw Reiner through the open window in the yard, loading the cattle. The dust swirled as farmhands ran alongside them, encouraging the unwilling beasts. Caroline wrinkled her nose and turned her head away. No wonder they were reluctant. She was quite sure they knew they were off to become someone's dinner. It was an awful thought — alive one minute and dead the next, at someone's whim!

She shuddered. She could never be a farmer's wife.

6

Reiner shifted his gaze from the auctioneer and focused on Caroline. Obviously desperate for shade, her slight figure drooped against the wall of a building, away from the noise and stench of the cattle. Even at a distance, he could see she was bored.

The auctioneer's high-powered voice ran on like a speeding train but their cattle had been sold. There was no necessity for Reiner to linger except that he and Josh had always hung around, enjoying the company after the solitude of the farm.

Still, the saleyards weren't the place for a woman. His companions had had little to say to Caroline this morning, offering their condolences in polite, stilted English, then becoming silent, bewitched no doubt by her appearance.

'How about I track down the solicitor

while you finish off here? I could meet you somewhere in the city,' she ventured.

He turned to find her at his shoulder. Somehow, she had edged her way toward him without him seeing.

'How will you get there?'

'Taxi,' she told him confidently.

He hesitated. There was no way he was going to let her talk to old man Kirkpatrick, not yet. He had too much ground to cover before she got near the truth. He raised his eyebrows.

'Do you think you can get one to go to the right place? Give me another minute or two,' he said when she didn't reply, 'and I promise I will be finished.'

She nodded, but he caught the exasperated twist of her mouth. He watched her retreat to the shade, thinking about that mouth and about how he longed to kiss it.

Reaching the wall, she turned, catching him staring at her. He swivelled his head rapidly back to the auctioneer, only to find himself pinned down by the man's hawk-like eyes, trapped. To move his head again now would be asking for trouble with the bidding!

He checked his watch surreptitiously. Thirty seconds passed then a minute, during which he thought he saw the flash of her camera lens out the corner of his eye. He tried to imagine how she would explain him to her friends, but that, although diverting, was painful. Her friends would be doctors, well-heeled and sophisticated, whereas he . . .

He glanced at his watch. The time was up, and he had successfully kept his mind off her mouth. He broke away from the crowd. Smiling, she came forward to meet him, stirring something in the pit of his stomach. He had made an effort with his appearance this morning, new jeans and a clean white shirt, but it wasn't just the clothes. He felt better. He was energetic.

She'd seen that straight off. At breakfast she'd stated, 'You're better. How's that possible?'

'The healing touch of a good woman,' he answered drily, pouring himself a coffee.

He knew how to rile her. He had worked that out fast.

'Aren't you the doctor?' he went on, as she choked on her toast.

'Doctors don't know everything,' she replied sharply after a gulp of coffee.

'You are right — they do not know everything. Do they know we must leave in ten minutes?'

'Why didn't you tell me? I've been awake for hours.'

'Why is that?'

He met her eyes over the rim of his mug, dying to know if her lack of sleep was due to anxiety about the farm's future.

'I don't know. I just couldn't get back to sleep. I've always been an early riser. The morning is the best part of the day.'

'Finally,' he said, 'we agree on something.'

Did they disagree on everything else?

It wasn't really that they disagreed. It was more that they were from totally different worlds. Did that mean she would never feel at home in his country?

She met him now, halfway across the saleyards, putting an end to his deliberations.

'At last I am done,' he told her with forced cheerfulness.

'Great,' she said.

Her smile had faded and her tone of voice told him she meant anything but.

'There is no need to sound so pleased,' he joked, but the blank look remained.

Perhaps he had been unduly unkind, keeping her waiting for so long.

'Something is wrong?'

'No,' she shrugged.

His irritation began to mount.

'You have been thinking this is all a waste of your time,' he guessed.

Women were all the same. He jammed one hand into his jeans' pocket and scuffed at the dirt with his boot.

'No, not at all.'

'Do not lie to me!'

He narrowed his gaze, and he saw by the flash in her eyes that he had her attention.

'I am not lying! If you must know, I was thinking about how different we were.'

He pushed his hat back. He had been so sure she was bored, and he had been wrong. That was a first.

'You think we are different?' he ventured.

'Of course. I live in a huge, busy city. You live quietly on a farm. It's like chalk and cheese.'

'It is not us who are different then, but our surroundings.'

She shrugged again. Impatiently, he pushed back a wayward strand of hair. So what if they were different? Why was it occupying so much of his time? Because it was important, he realised.

He could never persuade her to stay if her surroundings were alien, if she didn't feel at home. He moistened his lips. Since when had he wanted her to stay? He couldn't find an answer to that, but how else was he going to keep his farm? He didn't have anything to offer her that she didn't already have.

'Did you get a good price for the cattle?'

Her question snapped him back to the present.

'Not bad. I was tempted to buy some youngsters but then I remembered it was no longer my decision.'

He turned away, recalling the times he and Josh had chosen cattle together and feeling the man's loss more acutely than ever.

'How old were you when you came to live with my father, Reiner?'

He forced a grin.

'Always you have the questions,' he mimicked. 'Come,' he said, taking her hand, 'let us find a taxi.'

Holding her hand had the desired effect. It silenced her. But he'd forgotten its softness, forgotten its tendency to distract him. He couldn't risk that happening again. He needed to keep his wits about him.

The taxi's bright colour had faded to dirty lemon and heat suffused its interior. Reiner was accustomed to these things, but one glance at Caroline's wrinkled nose as she slid into the dusty seat told him she was not.

They had gone only a brief distance when they stopped for another two passengers, and Caroline had to shift position. He laid his arm along the back of the seat to give her shoulders room, but when a fourth person squeezed into the back and they all had to shift up once more, Reiner's hand went around her shoulders and rested loosely on her skin. He told himself it meant nothing. There was simply no room for him to place it anywhere else.

'Is it always like this?' she murmured.

'How would I know? I have never been in love.'

From where had that answer appeared! And why was he lying, shutting out those years with Lorna? He didn't dwell on it, but edged his mouth toward her ear.

'I meant the taxi,' she said primly.

'I know what you meant,' he said, breathing in.

She smelt delicious, like roses in hot sun.

'You must have been in love,' she whispered.

He drew back. She was persistent.

'I have been in love,' he said at last. 'Have you?'

She nodded briefly.

'It was a disaster.'

'A doctor?'

'No.'

She closed her eyes. He could see she didn't want to talk about it. He understood that, but he could be persistent, too.

'A patient?'

She nodded.

'I thought you were not allowed to fall in love with your patients.'

'That's only a theory, and he wasn't actually my patient.'

The sentence held an air of finality that suited him. There was nothing further he wanted to know. No doubt the man had broken a leg or something. The tips of his fingers caressed her skin, skin that was smooth, soft and warm. What had happened to his resolution to keep his distance?

'What was wrong with him?'

The question came out of nowhere!

'He had Aids,' she said, turning her face away.

They rode the remainder of the way in silence. Even if he had wanted to talk, he would have found it difficult to get the words out.

In the city, Reiner gave some instructions to the driver, and a few moments later the taxi deposited them in a busy main street. Caroline gazed around at the sprawling, low-set buildings, the pavements filled with the colour and bustle of Africans going about their daily business, which Reiner took for granted.

'This is it,' he told her, pausing

outside the entrance to one of the more impressive-looking buildings. 'But they may be closed for lunch.'

He glanced at his watch. If he had timed it right, they would definitely be closed for lunch. He had better have timed it right or he would be in all sorts of trouble.

'Not again.'

Caroline snapped her camera strap over her shoulder, the gesture showing her irritation.

'The last time I called the office was closed and they never came back. Doesn't anybody do any work around here?'

'Everybody goes home for lunch here,' he explained patiently. 'Most people live on the outskirts of the city and they can be home in five minutes. A simple meal with the wife and back in the office by two.'

'You're kidding,' she said.

'I am perfectly serious. Come on, let us find out.'

He hoped Kirkpatrick was a man of

habit. Leading the way into the building, he led her into the lift. Very soon they stood outside the offices of Lorentz & Kane, which were decidedly shut. He wiped the slight film of perspiration from his forehead. It was what the English would call a close shave.

'We'll come back after lunch,' she said.

'Better still,' he said, 'let me take you to lunch. I know a place where they serve the best steak you have ever tasted.'

With a bit of luck, she would have a few beers and forget about the solicitor!

'Steak?' she said dubiously.

'Ja, steak. Do not tell me you do not like steak.'

In the lift, he pressed a button and they began to descend. He realised he was hungry. Was he getting better? He glanced across at Caroline. The anxious expression on her face irked him. Did she think Australia was the only place where you could get a good steak? His country wasn't known only for its diamonds and wild-life. She would discover that, if he could get her to stay.

The lift jerked to a halt and two willowy African girls entered, office girls. He moved, making room for them, but they stood one either side of him, whispering and giggling in low monotones, and glancing shyly at him. He might not have been with a woman for a long time but he could recognise flirting when he saw it.

He quashed a grin and glanced in Caroline's direction. He hoped she was paying attention.

She was, but he couldn't read the expression on her face. He was too out of practice at that. Shrugging her shoulders, she smiled nonchalantly, wiping the smirk off his face. She wasn't the least bit perturbed by all the attention he was receiving!

The restaurant was busy when they arrived, but Werner, the owner, greeted Reiner with warmth and affection and found him a table without undue fuss.

'Do you come here often?' Caroline asked as they were seated and handed menus.

'Yes. It is a bad habit. Josh, your father, preferred to go to the club, full of journalists and gossip.'

'My father liked to gossip?'

He laughed.

'I did not say that. He liked to know what was going on in the world.'

The waitress approached and drew a notepad out of the frilly white apron covering her national dress. Reiner smiled in greeting. In Werner's restaurant you could be in Europe, except that outside the window the sky was too blue, the light too bright.

'Shall I order for you?' he asked Caroline.

'No. I know what I want. I'll have the risotto.'

'Risotto?'

His reaction was automatic.

'The risotto is very nice, but I have brought you here to have steak.'

'I am sure the steak is excellent, but

risotto will do me just fine,' she said firmly.

It was as he thought. He turned to the waitress, two fingers beating a restless tattoo on the tablecloth.

'She will have a steak. Make it two.'

'Don't ever tell me what I will or will not do,' Caroline interrupted sharply, leaning forward to get his attention.

His fingers jerked to a halt mid-beat. What was her problem?

'I don't eat steak, Reiner,' she said quietly.

'What do you mean?'

'I mean, I'm a vegetarian.'

He opened his mouth then closed it again. She didn't eat meat! Ten to one Josh had never known that when he'd made his will. He felt anxiety pull at the corners of his lips. Could the situation get any worse?

Yes, it could. She could sell the farm. She could find old man Kirkpatrick in when they returned to the office.

The waitress tapped her pad discreetly and Caroline turned and murmured to her.

'And how would you like your steak, sir?'

'Medium-rare,' he said absently.

He needed a drink. His nerves were shot. He glanced at Caroline.

'Can I order you a beer, or will I get into trouble for that, too?'

'I'd love a beer,' she said, then politely excused herself to wash her hands.

He left the table as well, ordering the beers on the way.

Scrubbing his hands, he wondered how he would get through the steak. If he didn't finish his meal, she would remember his need to see a doctor. He didn't have time to bother with doctors today. He had too much to think about.

'What's the preoccupation with all things German here?' she asked later as she sipped at her beer.

He looked up from his drink. He had been forgetting to make small-talk. What would she think?

'After the First and Second World Wars, a number of Germans migrated to Southern Africa, as the English did to your country. A large number of them settled here and carried on their traditions, German pubs and German schools. They are outnumbered now by the locals but the traditions go on.'

'And your father came out then, too?'

'Ja,' he replied curtly.

How had they got on to his father? He had thought the topic harmless enough.

'And where is your father now? What happened to him?' she asked softly.

'He is dead,' he said bluntly.

Would she stop asking questions now? What was he to say if she asked him what his father did for a living? Oh, he beat me up whenever he was bored. Once he . . .

His throat dried up. Was there any way out of this? There was. He took a swig of beer.

'Your father, Josh, why do you dislike him so much?' he said.

'You want me to talk about my father so that we can forget about your father?'

The waitress appeared with their meals and saved him from having to answer.

'I loved my father, Reiner,' Caroline said when the waitress left. 'It was he who evidently didn't like us.'

What could he say to that? He picked up his knife and fork.

'Bon appetit.'

Caroline took a mouthful of food and then after a minute she said, 'There's nothing really to tell. He just upped and went. I was left to care for my mother, an alcoholic, and my brother. When I went to university, there was never enough money. My mother was drunk most of the time, and when she wasn't, she was depressed. And then my brother — '

She broke off and laid down her fork, rattling it against her plate. Her hand was shaking and he fought down an urge to cover it with his own.

'Did my father ever tell you why he left us?' she said eventually.

'He did not talk about it.'

'Can you see then why I'm upset? Sixteen years and not a word, not even a postcard!'

He got through his steak although he thought at one stage that he might be sick. Caroline didn't finish her meal, which didn't surprise him. But her sudden cheerful voice did.

'Would you like a coffee? If the meal is anything to go by, I'm sure they make delicious coffee.'

He took the hint and smiled.

'You and your coffee,' he teased. 'We will have to grow some to keep you in stock.'

Idiot! Why had he said that? He clenched his hand around his beer glass.

'I know you cannot stay. Wrong thing to say. I do not think I can grow coffee, either. The climate is not right.'

She lowered her head and dabbed at her mouth with her napkin.

'I don't know. Your tomatoes are pretty impressive. Why don't you try? Start with a couple of bushes as an experiment.'

Suddenly he couldn't wait any longer. The tedium of the meal had sapped his energy as well as his patience.

'What is the point if you are going to sell the farm?'

'Am I going to sell the farm?'

'What else will you do with it?'

He shot the words at her, every muscle in his body tight. Where would he go if she sold the farm — his farm? He saw her mouth move. Had she said something or was he beyond comprehension? He felt like shaking her.

'Does nothing your father did matter to you?'

'It matters a great deal,' she said softly. 'I . . . '

She tailed off, her eyes filling with tears.

What was it she had been going to say? He turned his head away. He couldn't bear to see her cry. He had been unkind, impatient and rude. He patted his hip pocket. Did he have a handkerchief?

'I thought you said you didn't discuss this type of business with lunch!'

Startled, he raised his head as she threw down her napkin and glared at him, the tears under control.

He rose abruptly.

'Lunch is over,' he muttered.

7

At the offices of Lorentz & Kane, Mr Kirkpatrick's secretary offered her apologies and told Caroline he was out of town. There was no chance of seeing him until the following morning.

Caroline cursed under her breath and caught Reiner's stern look of disapproval. She was sick to death of being on her best behaviour. Who was he to stop her from venting her feelings and how was she ever going to sort this out if she could never speak with the solicitor?

'Couldn't we stay overnight somewhere?' Caroline reasoned.

'Make an appointment to see him first thing in the morning?'

'No.'

Reiner turned on his heel as if he couldn't wait to be out of there.

'What if Francina goes into labour? I

need to be on the farm.'

Out in the street, he stepped off the pavement and flagged down a taxi. Why did she have this niggling feeling he was relieved the solicitor was unavailable? What could the solicitor have told her that he didn't want her to know?

Back at the parked trailer, she clambered up into the overheated cabin.

'Now for the tyre,' she said, reading from her shopping list.

'You have a list?'

'Of course I have a list,' she snapped, winding down her window and longing for a stiff, bracing breeze.

If he hadn't picked up she was scatterbrained, she wasn't about to enlighten him. Lists were essential to her being organised!

They found a tyre company, and she rang the rental agency. After some negotiation they agreed to replace the shredded tyre, and while she waited for the paperwork to be done, Reiner bought a can of soft drink from a self-serve machine. He quenched his thirst then offered the remainder to her.

'Oh, heck!' she said with feeling. 'We've still got to get you to a doctor for a blood test and tetanus injection.'

That hadn't been on her list! He threw back his head and downed the remaining drink.

'You remembered! I was hoping you'd forget.'

She poked him playfully in the ribs and smiled as he squirmed away from her and laughingly fought off her hands.

The doctor's surgery was on the outskirts of town, but even with a reduction in traffic, parking the cumbersome trailer was no easy task. Caroline got out to direct Reiner, but all the same, she was amazed by his dexterity.

'How do you do it?' she asked as they seated themselves in the doctor's waiting-room. 'I mean, park the truck,' she added hurriedly.

'Practice. I've been driving one since

I could reach the pedals.'

Leaning forward, he rested his elbows on his knees.

'Your father taught you,' Caroline deduced. 'Was he a good teacher, like mine?'

'It was probably the only good thing he ever did,' he said, turning his attention to a pile of magazines.

Reiner turned a page as an elderly, bearded man with a stethoscope around his neck entered the reception area and studied Caroline over the rims of his glasses.

'Ah, Reiner,' he said, shifting his gaze to the man at her side.

He was gone at least ten minutes. Caroline picked up two glossy magazines but didn't take in any of the contents. Reiner's comments about his father occupied her mind. What a thing to say about your own father, not that she had much room to talk.

He returned at last, and they went out of the doctor's surgery together.

'Well?' Caroline said.

'He thinks I've got hypo - hypo . . . '

He paused on the stair and fumbled in his pocket, pulling out a scrap of paper.

'Hypoglycaemia,' he read out.

Hypoglycaemia? Of course! She ran her tongue over her lips. She must be slipping. How could she not have considered that possibility? It was glaringly obvious.

'So you were wrong. It is not glandular fever.'

'I was wrong,' she agreed quietly, frowning and catching her lower lip between her teeth.

'You never said you were perfect, although you may have thought it,' he quipped.

Too preoccupied to respond to his teasing, she asked, 'Have you had your tetanus shot? Did he take blood, and tell you how to manage your illness?'

'Relax,' he told her. 'Yes, to all three. The results will be available the day after tomorrow, but what exactly is hypoglycaemia?'

'You mean he didn't explain it to you?'

Caroline raised her eyebrows. She always explained everything to her patients in layman's terms, falling behind schedule sometimes to ensure they understood their illnesses.

'Can't be much of a doctor.'

It was her turn to tease.

'He was your father's doctor.'

'My father's doctor?'

If only she had known, she might have . . . She might have what — asked him how he could let her father die before she reached him?

'He said to tell you any time you want to talk, to drop in.'

Caroline chewed on her lip again. She would like that.

'Hypoglycaemia?' Reiner reminded her, and he seemed anxious.

She collected her thoughts.

'Well, it's basically low blood sugar.'

'Yes, but what does it mean? Is it contagious? Will I be able to kiss you again?' he blurted out.

'Again?' she said tartly. 'Did I miss something here? You haven't kissed me at all, yet.'

'I know, but I've wanted to.'

She dragged her gaze away from the slow, seductive smile spreading across his face.

'You asked me about hypoglycaemia,' she said pulling herself together with effort. 'Your body needs a certain amount of sugar to function effectively. When you're not eating properly, obviously that balance is not maintained, and your body . . . '

She was still talking when they strolled past a pharmacy. She stopped.

'I have to go in here,' she told him, nodding her head toward the shop.

'Fine, I will come with you.'

He listened attentively as she asked the pharmacist for needles, raised his eyebrows at the request for local anaesthetic, and eyed her purchases as she paid with her credit card.

'Who is this for?' he asked, indicating a bright yellow toy tractor she had found alongside the baby's bottles.

It wasn't quite what she was looking for. In truth, she hadn't been looking for anything.

'The little boy with the T-shirt, the one that says Nike across the front,' she said, drawing a thumb and finger across her chest to explain the lettering.

'Be careful you do not become attached. The boy has no mother.'

Her stomach clenched. She wished he hadn't imparted that snippet of information, or had he deliberately done so? Did he want her to become attached to the little boy, so that she wouldn't leave? With his studied air of indifference, it was hard to tell.

'What happened to his mother?' she asked once they were outside the pharmacy.

'She died. She had a breathing difficulty. Asthma, I think you call it.'

'Who looks after him?'

'We all do.'

They walked toward the trailer in silence. Reiner paused at the door, took off his hat and fiddled with the brim.

'I have been wrong,' he said quietly. 'I thought . . . '

He stopped, twisting the hat brim in his hands.

'I think you are a very good doctor,' he ended abruptly.

He ferreted in his pocket and drew out some keys. He tossed them over to her.

'Now, let us look at your driving skills. Yes? The doctor says I should not be driving.'

She caught the keys neatly. What had he been about to say — that he thought she was a useless doctor? And when had he formulated that opinion?

But there was no time to ponder. He was standing at the side of the truck, waiting. She swallowed. She was going to have to drive!

She tilted her head and peered down the length of the trailer, fighting an urge to walk away.

'Come on,' he encouraged, sensing her hesitation and taking her packages from her. 'It will be a piece of tart.'

'Cake,' she corrected, as she clambered up into the cabin. 'A piece of cake.'

★ ★ ★

When Caroline eventually drove up the farm's driveway it was dark, and she had been driving for the better part of the journey with the lights on. She parked the vehicle alongside Reiner's four-wheel drive and switched off the ignition. He left her without a word.

After a minute, she swung open the heavy door on her side and followed him. Jumping down from the high cabin, she found herself unexpectedly caught by strong arms. He had simply come round to assist her.

He smelled of dust and sun, and the tang of an orange he had peeled and shared with her in the cabin.

'You did not do too badly, for a beginner,' he murmured.

Smiling, she tilted up her face.

124

'Thank you for those few generous words. I really enjoyed my day, too.'

He shook his head.

'A dusty, dirty, smelly trip like that? It does not take much to make you happy, does it?'

She didn't answer. The truth was she couldn't remember the last time she had felt happier, more alive. How could she explain that?

'Good-night, Reiner,' she whispered.

It was late, and sometime tomorrow she must make preparations to leave. Her heart felt heavy at the prospect. She stepped forward, but she had nowhere to turn. He had braced a long arm against the side of the truck and hemmed her in between the door and himself.

She glanced up, wanting to see his eyes and his face, but they were just dark shadows. The chances were he was laughing at her as he had done on the drive home, not maliciously, but the gears would never be the same again! She ducked under his arm as he lowered his mouth to hers, the kiss glancing the side of her head.

Walking quickly toward her quarters, she didn't look back. It would be a mistake to look back, his arms had been so inviting.

She was almost at her door when he called out.

'Do not forget to check for snakes.'

She froze. Snakes! Why had he mentioned the word? With trembling fingers she turned the handle of the door and pushed gently on the wooden surface. She would not let him see how frightened she was.

Not venturing past the doorstep, she reached in, touched a switch, and light flooded the room. It appeared empty of anything sinuous and serpentine, but still she didn't enter. She cleared her throat, twice, then she stamped her dusty boots on the mat several times. Finally she took a tentative step over the threshold. Her gaze swept round the interior. She leaned over and flicked the edge of the doona — nothing.

From a corner of the room, she went down on all fours and peered under the bed. Something black and bulky stared back at her. She caught the scream before it got past her throat. It was her doctor's bag!

She walked the perimeter of the room, still nothing. She went across to the window and checked the sill. It was empty, but the yard wasn't. Through the open window, she saw Reiner in the moonlight, standing motionless beside the truck, watching her, waiting.

She drew the curtains with a deliberate swish, shutting out the sound of his voice and the feel of his hands. She found the bathroom door ajar, the interior in darkness. She kicked at the door and it flew open, then connected with something squashy. Caroline held her breath. The door swayed on its hinges. She inched forward and behind the door something slithered.

She didn't wait to discover what it was. She bolted, a scream choking on her lips. Her hands, damp with fear, slipped and fumbled on the door handle, but she got it open, and ran straight into Reiner's arms.

She screamed again.

He held her close to his chest, one hand splayed across her back, the other in her hair.

'You — you — '

'Sh,' he said. 'Sh.'

'I won't, I won't behave like you want me to! Why did you do that? Why did — '

'You think I put him in there? How could I? I have not been here, you know that. And if I wanted to frighten you, I would have put him in your bed.'

That didn't bear thinking about.

'Let me go,' she said, struggling out of his embrace.

He did, suddenly, and immediately she wanted to be in his arms again. They had been loving and comforting, and it had been too long since someone held her.

'I can't sleep in there,' she muttered, folding her arms across her chest. 'Isn't there somewhere else where I could sleep tonight?'

'Your father's room. He used it as a study, but the bed is made up.'

The voice was cold now, no trace of amusement or caring in it now.

'That'll be fine, thank you,' she said. 'Could you go back in there and get my things?'

She jerked her head toward her room. 'What do you need?'

She thought about her towel, her pyjamas, clean underwear for the morning — how was she going to send him in there for those intimate belongings?

'Couldn't you just remove him while I get my things?'

'He does not like to be handled too much.'

'Oh, all right. I need my towel, my toothbrush — just put everything that's in the bathroom into my toilet bag.'

He disappeared through the open door. She strained to hear his movements, hearing his footsteps go from the bedroom to the bathroom, the murmur of his voice — he talked to snakes! — and footsteps returning to her. He put her toilet bag and towel into her hands. In the half-light, he lifted an eyebrow.

'You do not wear pyjamas?'

'Of course I wear pyjamas!'

'I could not find any. You will have to go without, unless you want to look for them yourself.'

8

The heat of the morning had invaded the room when Caroline awoke. She groped for her watch. It was after nine and someone was knocking at the door.

'May I come in?'

She found her voice, answered in the affirmative, and pulled the covers up to her neck as Reiner came into the room, bearing a tray laden with bread rolls, jam, coffee, all the makings of breakfast. He put it down on the end of the big bed.

'I thought you said you were an early riser.'

'I am as a rule. I don't know what happened. I must have been exhausted.'

'A day like yesterday can be very tiring, all that sun. Coffee?'

'Love some.'

She raised herself into a sitting position, tucking the sheet under her armpits.

131

'I am not staying,' he told her, glancing at her efforts to cover herself. 'I have eaten, so do not worry.'

'I'm not worrying.'

His eyes glinted with amusement as if to say, who was she kidding? He poured milk into her coffee.

'Sugar?'

She nodded.

'You slept well?'

'Yes, thank you.'

He passed her the mug and their fingers touched. She settled it hastily on the bedside table before she spilled it. Why was she so jittery this morning?

'I am going to leave you in peace and see where Francina is,' he told her at the doorway. 'She hasn't come in this morning.'

'Let me know if there's anything I can do,' Caroline offered as he closed the door behind him.

After her coffee, wrapped in the sheet, she crossed to the bedroom's wardrobe and selected a shirt, similar to the one Reiner wore yesterday and almost as roomy. Obviously her father and Reiner bought from the same store.

Riffling still further, she found a pair of khaki shorts. They were far too wide in the waist, but she managed to belt them in loosely with a plait of leather. The belt wasn't secure by any means and it wasn't the most glamorous of outfits, but it would have to do.

On her father's desk, amongst the clutter of paperwork, stood a framed photograph. Crouched on a patch of grass, a boy with brilliant blue eyes and a faint gap between his top teeth smiled at her. Caroline sat at the desk. She leaned back in the upholstered chair and tried to imagine her father sitting there, sorting out bills, but before long her eyes were drawn back to the photograph. The boy was laughing, happy. Josh had obviously been a very good father figure to Reiner.

Why couldn't he have been a father to his own son? Paul had needed him so much. He had been the sort of kid who thrived on being needed. Caroline grimaced. She had tried to show Paul he was needed. She was still trying to show him.

A shout from outside caught her attention. She peered through the window. Reiner was jogging down the driveway toward the house.

'Caroline!'

The sound of her name coming from his lips startled her. She didn't think she had heard him use it before.

Hurriedly, she rose and crossed the room. With quick steps she moved down the passage, suddenly aware that the belt around the baggy shorts was nowhere near tight enough, but there was no time to worry about that. Reiner was coming in the front door, agitated.

'Caroline!'

The word erupted from his mouth. His wide-eyed gaze travelled rapidly up her body coming to rest on her face. Something was wrong. Something apart from her outfit.

He blinked and recovered his thoughts. 'The baby is coming, but Francina is bleeding, too much, I think. You must come.'

He stepped forward and, without ceremony, took hold of the plait of leather.

'But first, we must tighten these shorts or you will lose them. Then you will need your bag. You have found it again?'

As soon as they reached Francina's small house, Caroline set to. There was no time to be lost.

'I'd like clean sheets, towels and hot water,' Caroline told Reiner, pulling on plastic gloves. 'A clean apron would be good, too. Are you going to be all right?'

He stood awkwardly in the doorway of the small dwelling, his face ashen. Caroline gave him an encouraging smile.

'Everything's going to be fine. We'll manage, you'll see.'

He met her eyes and glanced in the direction of the bedroom where he had seen Francina lying on the room's narrow bed, breathing erratically. Then he turned and went outside.

Caroline put her head around the corner of the door as Francina drew breath after a long, drawn-out contraction, and Mathias, her husband, held up a glass of water to her lips.

'I'll be back in a mo,' she assured them.

She knew Francina and Mathias couldn't understand a word of her English but communication of any kind was important, and it was from her tone of voice that they would derive support.

'What's the matter?' she said outside to Reiner.

He thrust his hands into his pockets and kicked restlessly at a small stone.

'I remember what you told me, about Francina being small. Do you think something is not right?'

'I won't know until I've examined her, and if something is wrong, I won't tell her. The last thing I want is to cause her any stress.'

The palm of his hand touched her on the cheek. The gesture was unexpected and sudden and she wanted to lean her face into its warmth.

'She trusts you,' he said.

She met his eyes.

'I know, but that only makes it harder for me.'

'I will be back soon,' he told her. 'I will go now to get your list of things.'

Caroline returned to her patient and drew back the light sheet covering her. Divesting Francina of her traditional dress had been difficult but essential. She felt over the taut and swollen abdomen, grasping Francina's hand as another wave of pain gripped her.

When the contraction passed, Caroline did a quick internal examination, her brow creasing in a frown. Reiner had guessed correctly, something was amiss.

She left the bottom of the bed and moved to Francina's side. Giving her a bright smile and words of encouragement, she steadied her for another contraction.

Four more contractions passed before Reiner returned with a pile of linen. Nike was at his side, carrying a large basin and bucket for the hot water. The child gave her a shy smile, set down his load and scampered outside.

Caroline wiped her hands thoughtfully on a clean towel, and motioned for Reiner to step outside with her. She gave Francina and her husband another cheering smile, belying the sad news she was about to impart to Reiner outside.

'The baby's gone,' she said softly. 'I can't find a heartbeat.'

Reiner didn't reply. He averted his head but not before she saw his eyes, bright with emotion.

'I'm so sorry.'

Without thinking, she put her arms around him and hugged him.

'What about Francina?' he mumbled above her head.

She stepped away, but held on to him, wanting the warmth from his touch.

'We'll get her through this, but I'll need your help.'

'Of course,' he said, brushing the back of his hand across his eyes.

'Is the nearest hospital in the city?'

He nodded. That was one hundred and fifty kilometres away, the trip they had done yesterday. But Caroline didn't have time to think any further. A sharp and different cry from Francina had her hurrying back inside.

By lunchtime, the tiny, still form, a little girl, was swaddled and in her mother's arms, but Francina was weak and tired and losing blood.

Caroline pulled off her gloves and gratefully took the cup of coffee Reiner held out to her.

'I'm worried about her,' she told him quietly. 'She's lost a lot of blood and I can't seem to stop it. I'm going to drive her to the hospital.'

'I will come with you. You cannot go alone.'

'We'll need blankets for the back seat, one under her and one on top, towels, water . . . '

She sipped at the sweet, hot coffee, mentally running through a checklist.

'Oh, and phone the hospital and tell them we're on our way, and that in all likelihood she'll need a transfusion. Have you any idea what Francina's blood type is?'

'They will have a record of it. Josh and my mother took her for regular check-ups.'

'That was kind of them.'

He shrugged.

'Francina is like family,' he said huskily. 'I will bring the four-wheel drive around. Do you need anything else?'

'Yes. I need you to check my room for that snake as I must change.'

'That would be a good idea,' he said, smiling faintly. 'Anything else?'

'Just you,' she said absently, turning away to return to Francina.

In her room, changing quickly, the words echoed in her head — just you. How was it possible that in two days she could grow to need a man? She hesitated, one foot poised in the air over a clean pair of shorts. Did she need him?

She jammed her foot down hard on to the floor. No, she didn't!

Somehow she would go on with her life in Australia knowing he was on the other side of the world. It wouldn't make any difference. She hadn't fallen in love with him. The idea was preposterous.

In the drive on the way to the city hospital, she told herself she was being ridiculous. Soon she would be back in Melbourne and all this would be behind her, faint and dim, like a dream — a dream of walking down a dusty driveway and into a man's life.

She would get her promotion when she got home, begin Paul on his rehabilitation and life would carry on. She would have no regrets about leaving. She glanced over her shoulder at Francina curled up on the back seat with her head on her husband's lap.

They would get through this. There would be other babies.

And Reiner?

He would remain elusive. She would remember him only as the man she almost came to know, almost came to love. But what would she do with the farm?

She clenched her jaw, her eyes brimming with tears. Stop it, she told herself, stop it!

★ ★ ★

It was after midnight when they returned home. They had left Francina at the hospital, settled and out of immediate danger. Her husband would spend the night by her side and move to the town in the morning to stay with friends.

As they went up the veranda stairs, Reiner reached across and took Caroline's hand. His touch was warm and oddly comforting.

'Tired? You must be.'

'Hmm.'

She stifled a yawn. She had driven there and back, assisted with Francina's complications, and stayed to help with another patient who had been involved in a car accident. Were it not for Reiner's insistence that they should return home, she would still be there. She could see that the hospital was horribly short-staffed.

The phone rang as they reached the top step.

'Go,' she said, disengaging her hand, reluctantly, hoping it wasn't bad news, though she was quite sure Francina was going to be fine.

In the kitchen, she filled the kettle and set out the coffee mugs. She walked out on to the veranda with the tray just as Reiner called her from the passage.

'It is my mother, phoning from Germany,' he announced. 'She forgets the time difference. She wants to greet you.'

Caroline took the phone from him. Turning, he mouthed something at her.

Caroline frowned, not understanding. She wasn't paying attention. She was thinking that if anybody would know what her father had wanted, surely it would be this woman.

'Hello, Caroline Carter.'

A moment's hesitation followed.

Then, 'Here is Liesl, I am so pleased to meet you. Your father — '

Her voice broke and she drew breath.

'Your father would be so very happy to know we are speaking together. Reiner, he was not so sure you would come but I knew you would not let your father down. I could tell your father was proud even though he leaves you so many years ago. He always knew what his daughter was doing. I know his daughter will be like him.'

Caroline mumbled something in response. How could her father have already known what she was doing? Unbelievably, tears were sliding down her cheeks.

'And you are sleeping in the house, in the room close by Reiner's, are you not?

Do you like it? It is so pretty with the big double bed and lace at the windows. I want you to be comfortable. And now you have gone all quiet because I have been doing too much talking.'

She paused.

'Are you still there, Caroline?'

Caroline sniffed and wiped her eyes with a corner of her shirt.

'I am still here,' she said, but her voice wobbled.

She drew breath and got her emotions under control.

'Maybe this is the wrong time to ask you, Leisl, but I haven't had a chance to speak to the solicitor. I need to know if my father provided adequately for you.'

'Oh, ja. There is not need for worry there. Your father transferred his funds into my account when he first became ill. He is a very generous man.'

Caroline smiled weakly.

'Good. Then I can leave knowing — '

'Leave!' Liesl's voice rose. 'But,

Caroline, you only just arrived. You cannot leave.'

Caroline's face puckered with emotion. She wanted to say she would try to keep the farm. She had wanted to say that to Reiner yesterday, but how could she keep a farm in Africa when she lived in Australia? She could never make commitments to run a farm, forego the promotion she had worked long and hard for, the increase in salary. Then there was Paul.

'I must leave,' she answered. 'I have a life in Melbourne, a career, a brother.'

'Brothers can be fixed. Bring him to the farm. He can help Reiner.'

Paul help Reiner? It wasn't such a crazy idea. Paul would love the farm. He had always shown an affinity with animals and he was good at practical work, like fixing fences, growing tomatoes.

'But this career,' Leisl continued, 'this is more important?'

'Yes.'

But was it? Caroline frowned and

wound the telephone cord around her fingers.

'What did my father want me to do with the farm, Leisl?'

Liesl remained silent.

'This is not easy for me,' she said at last. 'I tell Josh to write a letter, but he say is not necessary, you will know what to do.'

That was just it. She didn't. Caroline jerked her hand free of the cord and ran it through her hair in exasperation. How was she supposed to work this out?

'Reiner tells me you are taking good care of Francina and the baby. Thank you.'

This was what Reiner had been trying to signal to her! He hadn't told his mother about the baby. He didn't want to upset her. He really was a thoughtful son.

'You will not mind if I stay here longer, will you? This visit of mine, it helps to keep the tears away.'

'Of course we won't mind,' Caroline

told her. 'Take your time. We will see you when you are ready to return.'

What was she talking about? She would be long gone by the time Liesl returned, back in Australia, in Melbourne, doing her rounds in her crisp white coat in her clean, clinical hospital, spending hours behind her desk with only paperwork and the cold gold lettering on her door, that read **Deputy Head of Paediatrics**, for company.

There was nothing more to say. With an effort, Caroline said goodbye, feeling more confused than ever. Her head was thinking one way and her heart acting another.

9

Reiner uncorked a bottle of red wine and let it breathe. Flicking off the veranda light, he surveyed the scene. Romance was one thing, but this was too dark, he decided. He needed to see Caroline's face. Fetching a candle from the kitchen, he stuck it into an old wine bottle and was lighting the wick when she came through the doorway.

She eased herself into a wicker chair and, with an audible sigh, closed her eyes. She looked exhausted. He longed to go to her and take her in his arms, kiss away the sadness he saw etched on her face, but he must not rush things. He knew now what Josh had intended when he left her the farm, but there was a danger she hadn't a clue. How would she react to the idea of running a clinic on the farm?

'Caroline?'

He used her name again. Something about the way it rolled off his tongue made him want to say it again and again. So much for his resolution.

She opened one eye, and he held out the bottle of wine in silent invitation. She nodded.

While he was pouring the liquid and concentrating on not spilling, she said, 'Reiner, why did you put me out in the guest quarters when I arrived? Your mother says she prepared a room in the house in case I arrived.'

He pushed a glass across to her. What could he say? How did he tell her that because the room was alongside his, he didn't trust himself?

'I have not . . . ' he began and petered out, but she didn't complete his sentence for him this time, so he would have to spit it out.

'I did not want to like you,' he said finally.

'I gathered that much.'

'There is another reason,' he went on before he lost his nerve. 'There has not been a woman in my life for some time. I was not sure if I still knew what to do, I mean, how to behave.'

He spread his hands in a helpless gesture. He was making a real mess of this, just as Lorna had made a real mess of him. He hadn't cared if he lived or died. With surprise, he realised he had changed. He now had so much to live for.

She sipped at her wine. He wished she would say something. She had never been at a loss for words before. What had his mother said to her to make her so quiet, or was it something of his doing?

'I needed a drink tonight,' he said unnecessarily. 'I will not sleep without it. You are probably used to these things.'

'You never get used to death, Reiner,' she said softly, meeting his eyes over the top of her glass.

He averted his eyes, scared that he would do something out of character if he gazed into her hazel eyes for too long.

'Have you ever lost anybody?' he asked.

He could see the question took her by surprise and he ran his hand anxiously over the back of his neck.

'I am not coping very well with what has happened,' he said, making an excuse for suddenly wanting to know everything about her. 'It has been too soon after . . . '

'After my father's death?'

'Ja.'

'It takes time to get over a death, two to three years, sometimes more. I know. Neil, the man I married, he died.'

She put her hand up to her mouth as if it had been a mistake to blurt that out. But he wanted her to keep talking.

'Yesterday, in the taxi, you said it had been a disaster,' he encouraged gently.

'That's not what I meant. That sounds like I don't care that he died. It wasn't like that. I did care, but he didn't love me.'

She fiddled with the stem of the wine glass. Then she went on.

'When I married him, he was dying. He pretended he loved me so that he could get what he wanted which was proper medical attention, day and night.'

'You knew he was dying?'

'I knew, but I thought he loved me. I had never been in love before. I thought — '

She shook her head.

'He used me,' she said finally.

'When did you find out?'

'The day after we were married, on our honeymoon. He said something cruel, and I realised — '

She broke off again. Her voice wobbled.

'But you went ahead anyway, and nursed him until he died?'

Anger sliced into his voice. How could some man have put her through that?

'Yes, of course I did,' she said fiercely, turning to him, her eyes filling with tears. 'I couldn't walk away. I had undertaken to love him, care for him, until death did us part.'

'And you never break a promise.'

He put down his wine glass before it shattered in his hand. Stiff-legged, he rose and stepped away from his chair, crashing clumsily against the side of the table.

The wickerwork clattered on the floor and the wine bottle teetered. He made it to the veranda's steps but stopped short of the edge, his hands clenched at his sides.

How could he tell her he loved her now, and in the next day or two break the news that the farm had once been his? How could he explain that loving her and wanting his farm back were two separate things? Could he convince her that he wasn't using her just as her ex-husband had done? He didn't think so.

However, he had to tell her about the farm. If he withheld that information and she discovered the truth, as she inevitably would, how would he face her? How would he convince her that he loved her, that he would have loved her anyhow, regardless of any farm?

'I must leave in the morning.'

Her husky voice reached him as though she spoke through fog. He realised she had risen from her chair.

'I cannot stay any longer.'

Stunned, he turned. She couldn't go. When would he tell her how he felt? How would he tell her?

'I have to attend to a certain small boy's arm first, and then I will be on my way.'

She started toward him.

For one wild moment he thought she was going to kiss him goodbye, but then he realised she had to pass him to reach the steps.

All he had to do was put out his arms. But he couldn't. He couldn't bring himself to stop her. There was nothing he could offer her that she didn't already have.

Was that why he was incapable of speaking up? Was he terrified of being rejected a second time?

She halted alongside him. He couldn't take his eyes off her, but she didn't look at him and he knew why. He had shown not one iota of compassion toward her.

She stumbled as she went down the steps, and, too late, his arm jerked out to stop her.

But she didn't see it, and she didn't look back. All too quickly, she moved past the thorn tree, across the patch of grass toward the guest quarters, and into the darkness.

★   ★   ★

She set her alarm for five and woke before the sky became tinged with pink. Opening her door to let in the fresh, morning air, she found her little friend on the doorstep, his head resting on his arms, waiting. How had he known she was leaving?

With the interlude of time, his wound was healing nicely she discovered, and no longer required stitching. She dressed it again, and gave him his present with the minimum of fuss, almost shoving him out the door.

Then she packed quickly, keeping her mind occupied by folding all her shirts into squares methodically, which was most unlike her. The feel of a small boy's warm arms around her neck as he hugged her goodbye would take a long time to fade.

Clutching her bags, she walked over to the farmhouse. The hire car's shredded tyre had been replaced by one of the farm employees while they were at the hospital, and the vehicle now stood at the side of the driveway, ready to go.

She climbed the steps of the veranda and turned, looking out over the farm, past the handkerchief of green grass, down the dusty driveway, into the distance. Barren and desolate, with little greenery, no trees to speak of, there was nothing in the distance.

Nothing — and there was nothing to keep her here, either. Why then, was she reluctant to go? Was it because someone had put an idea into her head about Paul, and something had happened to her heart, something to do with a little brown-skinned kid, a stillborn baby, and an unfathomable man?

With an effort, she heaved her luggage on to the back seat and got in. One of the farm dogs padded down the driveway, but apart from that, she saw no-one.

At the airport, she returned the hired car with some terse words about the state of the spare tyre, and checked in her luggage. Then she ordered coffee and took it into the lounge, choosing a seat that gave her a good view of the airport's entrance. She wasn't expecting anybody. She merely wanted to see who was coming and going.

Halfway through her coffee, a large woman settled herself into the seat alongside hers.

'Excuse me,' she said, 'I couldn't help noticing you from where I was sitting.

You wouldn't be Josh Carter's daughter, would you?'

Caroline nodded. Was she so much like her father that people could recognise her across a crowded room?

'I thought so. I saw the Australian sticker on your suitcase when you checked in your luggage, and, well, the likeness is hard to miss.'

Caroline stirred her coffee needlessly. She didn't want to converse with anyone. She wanted to be alone with her thoughts. How would she get rid of this busybody?

'I was standing in the queue behind you,' the woman went on, 'but I could see you were in a world of your own. Hard to lose a father, at any time. My sympathy. What a pity you're going home. The family will miss you.'

'You know the family?'

'Ja, I've lived in the area for years. Your father was the best thing that happened to them, but then you'd know all about it.'

Caroline's fingers tightened around

her cup. She took a deep breath.

'I don't actually. I don't know all about it.'

'You don't?'

The woman gaped at her. She had a freckled, open face and, in spite of her desire to be alone, Caroline found herself warming to her.

'That would explain why you're leaving then,' she said thoughtfully. 'I suppose that seeing as you've made up your mind to go, there's no harm in telling you.'

'So the farm does have a secret,' Caroline murmured, as the woman shook out her skirt and rearranged herself in the chair.

'I suppose as far as you're concerned it has a secret, but everyone else round here knows the story. The farm is actually Reiner's. His father owned the farm originally. It never was your father's.'

Caroline swallowed, tried to say something but failed. Her mind in overdrive, she couldn't think straight, either. The farm was Reiner's?

'Schmidt owned a great deal of land but he lost it all through gambling, all of it, every last piece. The farm was the only thing he had left, and then your father turned up, out of the blue, nobody knows why or how, and went to work for Schmidt. He was a real tyrant, Schmidt. You know the kind, arrogant, moody. People say he used to beat Liesl. I don't know about that, but I saw him hit the boy once.'

Her voice dropped and she winced as if recalling every detail.

'Nobody ever took him in hand. People were too scared of his temper.'

The air crackled with static suddenly as the intercom system came on and Caroline heard her flight being called.

'Come on,' the woman said, easing her bulk from the chair, 'there's our plane. I'll tell you the rest on board.'

'You mean there's more?'

'Oh, yes.'

She looked at Caroline and shook her head helplessly.

161

'Something tells me you actually need this information before you board that plane.'

Caroline nodded, holding her breath.

'I wonder why he didn't tell you himself.'

Caroline breathed out.

'Tell me what?'

Picking up her handbag and small holdall, the woman instructed, 'Walk with me. We can talk as we go.'

Caroline slung the camera bag over her shoulder and fingered her boarding pass. What could this woman tell her that would possibly make a difference?

'When we heard that Josh had won the farm off Schmidt, nobody believed it. Josh was such a straight, hard-working man, not the sort of man you would associate with gambling. But the next thing we knew, Schmidt had cleared off. He died within six months, had a heart attack apparently. Some people say Josh planned the whole thing. You know, rescuing the boy and his mother, and took the biggest gamble of his life.'

They had reached the boarding queue. Caroline could see the plane parked out on the runway.

'And Reiner? Something happened to him, didn't it?'

Her voice was a whisper.

'Let's face it,' the woman continued, leaning in confidingly toward her, 'he had a bad time. He was engaged to be married, two years ago. But when the girl heard the farm belonged to Josh and that he wasn't Reiner's real father, she broke off the engagement, four days before the wedding!'

She shook her head and edged forward in the queue.

'My daughter's expecting me in Sydney,' she announced, holding out her boarding pass. 'Married an Aussie, she did, only he farms crocodiles, not sheep or cattle. Crocodiles!'

She laughed, but her laughter died when she turned to Caroline.

'You're not coming, are you?'

'No, I'm not.'

Caroline's mouth parted in surprise at her own words.

'I can't go. There's something I haven't said.'

'Oh, dear. I was looking forward to your company. It's such a long trip.'

She reached the front of the queue and gave the flight attendant her pass. Caroline hung back. What was she doing? Had she completely lost the plot?

No! She was going to be her father's daughter and take the biggest risk of her life.

'Good luck,' the woman called over her shoulder as she disappeared through the doors.

Fumbling, Caroline picked up the pay phone back in the airport terminal. The phone number of the farm lay in front of her. She had the correct coins, but what would she say? Could she risk everything again for a man who might be using her, like Neil had done?

She put down the phone, dropping it

into the cradle. But was Reiner using her? He'd purposely not told her his history, not told her the farm was rightfully his, even when she'd threatened to sell it. He was waiting until she came to her own decision — which she still hadn't done! She had left him without telling him what she was going to do.

He must be living on a knife-edge.

* * *

She passed Reiner on the road back to the city. For a minute she wondered if her eyes were deceiving her, but the man at the wheel was all too familiar. In her rear-view mirror, the four-wheel drive was a blur. He was going 'way too fast. The fact that he was in a hurry gave her hope. Maybe he cared about her after all.

She knew he wouldn't have recognised her. He wasn't looking out for her as he thought she was getting on to a plane. The dust rose at the edge of the road as she made a desperate u-turn and went after him.

Just before the airport, she spotted him pulled off at the side of the road. She saw why. Her plane had taken off and was climbing into the clear blue atmosphere, Johannesburg, first stop, then Perth, Sydney, Melbourne and home.

She pulled in behind him and turned off the ignition. His head and arms were slumped over the steering-wheel, motionless. Did that mean he was ill again, or did he want her back? Love her? One thing at a time, Caroline!

She sat quietly in her car trying to get her thoughts together as the plane roared overhead.

Home — was your land of birth your home? Theoretically, yes, but she felt equally at home here, in this land her father had called home. Was she mad, giving up her career and her country? And for what?

Was it for Reiner she was doing it, or the people she'd met, or the land that was so desolate and barren it ached to look at it? Or were they all intertwined, inseparable?

A door slammed. Reiner stood in the road, the sleeves of his crisp, cotton shirt rolled back to the elbows. He had made an attempt to cut his hair, she noticed. It almost made her smile, but she was too nervous. When would he have had time to do that?

Caroline got out and they moved to the side of the road, standing awkwardly. The sand burned through her shoes and the heat pressed down on her. She had no idea what to say. She hadn't rehearsed a thing.

'I thought I'd lost you,' he said faintly.

There were dark circles under his eyes as if he hadn't slept at all. She tried to reply, but no words would come.

'What are you doing here?'

He brushed a strand of hair off his forehead impatiently.

'Someone told my story, yes? Everything about my father, the farm.'

'A large woman,' she murmured, 'with a daughter in Australia.'

'Mrs Hunter, the postmaster's wife. Knows everything about everybody.'

He thrust his hands into his pockets as if he didn't know what to do with them.

'I was coming to you,' he said, moving towards her as if to illustrate this, then stopped. 'I could not ask you to stay. It would have looked like I was using you. I had to let you make the decision.'

'Even if it meant I almost went away because I didn't think you cared?'

'I did not want your pity.'

'I have no pity for you, Reiner. If anything, I'm jealous. You had the father I never had.'

'I know how lucky I am,' he said.

He looked up at the sky, following the thin vapour trial of the plane.

'You are not on the plane,' he remarked.

'Sometimes people do inexplicable things.'

'But you are not inexplicable, Caroline. You are logical, you make lists. You are messy sometimes, too, but you would have a very good reason for turning back.'

I do have a reason, she wanted to say. You are the reason, but she couldn't get those words out, not yet.

'I was thinking . . . '

She tailed off, suddenly afraid to go on.

'Thinking what?'

'Could you build me a clinic on the farm? I think that's what my father wanted. I could stay and be a doctor for your people. I could stay and . . . '

She squinted up at his face in the sun.

'Does that sound like a good reason to you?'

'This is an excellent reason. I like it very much, but is that the only one?'

He was tentative.

'I have a brother, as you know,' she said hurriedly, anxious to reach the real reason. 'I want to bring him out here.

He needs special care.'

Later, she would tell him the details of what it was Paul needed.

'And these are the only two reasons you stayed behind?' he said.

'No, I mean yes, I mean — '

She drew breath. This was the hard part.

'I was thinking that maybe you and I . . . you and I could . . . '

'I have nothing to offer you.'

'You have everything to offer me,' she encouraged gently. 'Never underestimate yourself.'

Mentally, she ran through the list of his qualities, deleting most of the judgements she'd made on that first day.

'You're intelligent, funny, caring, unpredictable. I love your sense of humour, your blue eyes, the gap between your top front teeth.'

She stopped, waiting for him to laugh at her, but one look at his face told her there was no chance of that.

'You are flirting with me,' he

announced seriously.

He shifted his weight restlessly from one leg to the other. She realised he wanted to tell her something, something he was finding it hard to get out.

'There is a feeling when you dream badly. You fall through air and there is nothing to stop you. Do you know this feeling?'

She nodded.

'Believe me, we're both falling together,' she told him.

He grinned suddenly and closed the distance between them, taking her into his arms. She held him tightly and for a long moment they stood wordlessly together, his head bowed over hers, his heart beating wildly under her ear. She was afraid to let him go.

'From the moment I saw you,' he said hoarsely into her hair, 'I had a feeling we were meant to be together. But it did not make sense. I fought it all the way, and I was scared. I still am.'

She lifted her head from his chest and smiled. It was important that he saw her face, saw the truth and love in her eyes.

'There's nothing to be frightened of, Reiner. It's only me.'

'Only you?' he said quietly. 'I nearly lost you.'

'And I, you,' she admitted. 'My father took such a risk. What if I had never worked out the idea of the clinic? Would you have told me how you felt?'

She shook her head.

'Of course, you wouldn't have. When did you find out?'

'What, that I loved you or about the clinic?'

She grinned shyly.

'Both.'

'I will do the easy one first,' he said. 'The idea of a clinic has been growing since I took you to the sale yards. You looked so out of place, and yet I knew that a person with your skills would always be needed. And then, yesterday, Francina and the baby helped.'

His voice stammered slightly with

emotion. He tucked a curl of hair behind one of her ears.

'I loved you from the moment you woke me up the day you arrived, but it took a while for me to realise, and then I could not work out how you felt about me.'

'Oh, Reiner,' she said, 'was I so unapproachable?'

'Yes, you were,' he said simply. 'I wanted to tell you everything last night, but then I could not, not after what you told me. I was angry I could not share it with you because I knew you would go away, and there was nothing I could do to stop you.'

He took a shaky breath. He was talking as if he could not stop.

'I want a relationship with you like your father and my mother had. They told each other everything. But I need practice,' he admitted.

He smiled, revealing the sensuous gap between his front teeth.

'I could not sleep last night. When I did, I woke up late and found you already had left. I was functioning on, what do you say, automatic pilot?'

'I noticed. You forgot to shave.'

'I did?'

He rubbed a thumb and forefinger pensively along his jaw-line.

'How could I forget? I needed to put my best leg forward.'

'Best foot,' she corrected.

'Best foot, best leg, what does it matter?'

'It matters a great deal. It's not good English.'

'You are not going to argue with me, are you?' he teased, but he was gazing at her with love in his eyes.

'No, not now. We have the rest of our lives for that.'

'Good, because I want to kiss you,' he said quietly, his gaze lingering on her mouth, 'I have been wanting to kiss you for days.'

She slid into the warmth of his welcoming arms once more and he kissed her, finally, under the hot, African sun. When they drew apart she was trembling, and she thought that of all the things her father had left her, this man was the most special bequest of all.

THE END